Something Hidden

Something Hidden

an anthology

Edited by Debz Hobbs-Wyatt and Gill James

Bridge House

British Library Cataloguing in Publication Data

A Record of this Publication is available from the British
Library

ISBN 978-1-907335-31-0

This edition published 2013 by Bridge House Publishing
Manchester, England

Contents

Introduction

The stories in the collection were all entries in our 2011 short story competition.

We asked for something a little darker this time and we certainly got that. Our talented writers managed to avoid descending into pure evil and nastiness. That isn't easy.

The endings are not upbeat but there is often some hope at the end. Will there be more people alive in the rubble? Will someone now recognise the signs of despair? The spell of childhood might be broken but at least it means you're growing up.

Some stories were incredibly sad but beautiful in that sadness. Some of the stories are gritty, some make you think and some challenge the placid veneer of calmness we see in life. Some do all of these things at once.

It was difficult choosing the winners from amongst these finely-crafted, thought-provoking short stories. We had to reject some other stories that were also pretty good. Those selected just had a little edge. They went just a little deeper and were written just that shade more tightly.

In the end we singled out Sarah Hegarty's *Something Hidden* for its rich but subtle story-telling. Sarah takes us on a journey but doesn't quite hold our hand all the way – the reader has to work with her to understand what is happening to Lorna.

As a very close second we chose Linda Flynn's *I Knew It in the Bath*. Clothed in beautiful language three stories weave together here: a tragedy, a back-story and a bath time.

We hope you will enjoy this collection. And if you think you would like to write for us, do look at what we say about our future plans at the end of the book.

Something Hidden

Sarah Hegarty

(The winner of our 2011 Short Story Competition)

For Fiona

"I know what we need," Max said, striding on to the patio one Friday evening in late July.

Lorna hadn't heard him come through the house. She had been listening for a different sound.

She peered out from under the parasol, flinching at the heat. Max's tie was undone, his greying hair flat with sweat, face flushed from the commuter train. Sun caught the beer glass in his hand. He smiled, and raised the glass at her, and Lorna saw an actor in a silent film, tightrope sliding under his polished shoes, the street falling away below.

Before he could explain what they needed, Max went back inside.

On the old wooden table the tub of ice cream Lorna and Toby had been sharing had turned to soup. All afternoon, until he'd gone in to watch TV, they'd been playing Snap. At times it had been as much as Lorna could do to lift a card and lay it on the wobbling pile. Stealing under the parasol the heat had butted up against her, nosing and insistent, like a badly-trained old dog, sniffing at the secret of her, hidden under her clothes.

She heard Max open the kitchen cupboard, and the chink of pudding bowls. But he must have thought better of it because he returned with only a packet of wet wipes, which he put next to her. Then he dragged over a fold-up chair.

"Sea air!" he said, as if he'd just invented it.

Lorna thought of consumptive Victorians trailing up

8

and down promenades. She lifted her thin cotton dress away from her sweaty stomach.

"A change of scene would do you good," Max added.

She tried not to hear the criticism in his words. Her mother had told her she needed to pull herself together. They shouldn't have left it so late – seven years was too big a gap. She was lucky to have the summer holidays off; she'd be fine by the start of term.

"Where would we go?" she asked. The cramped, airless house was suddenly a haven.

"Rich said we could have his place in Devon." Max touched her elbow. "Do you remember? We went there once, before Toby was born."

Lorna felt her throat constrict. "Great," she said.

On the journey, drifting in and out of sleep, Lorna tried and failed to picture the cottage. Max had said nothing more about their previous visit, and she couldn't remember a time when their days had been as free and weightless, the space between them full of promise.

Max drove into a narrow lane. The car brushed the overgrown hedgerow, shaking butterflies from the dog roses and wild clematis. At the end of the lane was the cottage, its windows gold in the evening sun. Lorna didn't recognise it.

"We're here!" Toby was scrambling out of his seat before Max had pulled up the handbrake.

Lorna pushed open the car door and hot air slid in. Barefoot, she stepped onto the scorched grass.

"It's wonderful here if you get the weather," Max kept saying.

His skin turned red-brown. Toby's face bloomed with freckles. Lorna dozed in the shade. Her limbs were soft,

9

liquid. The books she had brought to read lay untouched in a stack by the bed, in the room under the eaves.

Exhausted by the sea air, calmed by the cool evenings, Toby went to bed each night without protest. Max and Lorna sat in the small sitting room, under the dull yellow glow of the standard lamp, watching TV.

In the wide, cold bed Lorna let Max hold her, and tried to feel comforted.

At the supermarket on the other side of the estuary Max bought a hammock, which he strung between the apple trees in the small garden. Lorna understood it was to contain her. Wordlessly, they had settled into a routine. In the mornings they played with Toby: cards, or board games whose rules eluded her. In the afternoons Max and Toby went out.

"We'll leave you to rest," Max said, backing out of the gate.

She wanted to tell him the garden was far from restful: the heavy air was never still. Bees and wasps harassed her; swallows lined up on the telephone wire opposite, mocking her by their sheer numbers; butterflies batted the windowpanes, blundering their way inside. Above the trees, on the hill behind the cottage, a pair of buzzards circled and hung, pulled together and apart like magnets.

Lorna watched the buzzards until her eyes could barely make them out, until she saw them behind her eyelids. In the drift and swoop of their bodies she sensed a shared tenderness, something hidden, protected. She imagined the stretch of feathers as they took off, the lift of air under their wings.

One afternoon she woke, lurching from sleep, her dream clinging. The sense of the child had been vivid: skin against skin; a smell of milk. And a caress: delicate and light as air.

Slowly she remembered where she was. She felt the hammock under her, the warm air, heavy on her skin. But something had changed. A pulse beat in her throat.

She got up and wandered into the cool of the kitchen. The clock said three. Max and Toby would be out until five. She trailed up the twisting stairs, the dark wooden beams low over her head. The back of her neck, her underarms, even the backs of her knees were sticky with sweat. She peeled off her clothes. Heart pounding she twisted in front of the old, spotted mirror, straining to see her shoulder blades. She stretched her fingers up her back as far as she could, fingertips probing. There was no doubt.

When Max and Toby returned Lorna was back in her hammock, in the shade, a sundress covering her secret. Toby went indoors to watch TV and Max brought her a glass of wine and a small pottery bowl of olives.

"It's so peaceful here." He sat down next to her, slopping his beer on the ground. He shaded his eyes and looked up at the hill. "I hope – are you glad we came?"

The buzzards were back, circling over the trees. Lorna pressed her shoulders into the hammock.

"Sure." Soft, cool air flowed under her arms.

"It was a good idea to come, wasn't it?"

She heard the plea in his voice. "Yes. I love the – space."

"Toby – I think – he was worried about you. Well – we both were." Max reached across and patted her wrist.

"I know." She kicked the tree with her bare foot to make the hammock swing. She didn't look at him.

"Lorna."

11

"Mmm?" The buzzards approached each other then veered away.

"We can try again, you know. I mean, if – when you're up to it."

She needed him to go back inside the house.

"Lorna?" Max stretched out of his seat to peer under her sunhat. She almost expected him to lift her sunglasses.

"I've changed, Max." She kept her gaze on the hill.

"Of course you have. We all have."

That night Lorna flew, high up. The jet stream was a solid rush of air under her feet. On her honey-gold wings she cruised through clouds, brushing their soft edges; swooped through red-streaked sunsets. Lazily she glided above tiny hills and rivers, houses scattered below her like children's bricks. Beside her the buzzard flew. In the curve of its wing was the small body. Lorna glimpsed dark hair. She touched the curled fist, and felt the fingers grip. In her chest her heart expanded, pushing at her ribs, bones fusing with the dream of flight.

When she grew tired she climbed onto the buzzard's back, pressing her legs into its silky feathers. Hooking her feet under its claws she felt blood, thick and warm, against her flesh.

She woke before dawn to feel the familiar stickiness on her thighs. She had forgotten that, under her treacherous skin, the process would be starting again.

The heat began to ease. Max said the wind had changed. One afternoon they went out together in the car, along the coast and over a new bridge. Toby, fidgeting with excitement in the back, kept pointing things out: a field of jostling sheep, or an oddly-shaped cloud. Lorna sat in the front next to Max, a cushion behind her shoulders.

On the way back, three paragliders were drifting in the early evening sky.

"It must be great, to fly by yourself," Toby said.

Lorna's heart snagged on his words. Instantly she saw the neat fields, far below; felt the rush of air under her arms.

"They don't do it by themselves, son." Max raised his voice above the engine noise. "They're towed up to high ground by a big car, like a Land Rover, then they let go."

"Oh."

Lorna heard Toby's disappointment. "But they still fly, Max!"

Back at the cottage Lorna hesitated in the garden. Excitement fluttered in her chest. She whispered to Toby.

"Yes!" he shouted.

Max, fiddling with the door key, turned round. "What is it?"

"We're going to do a project. Before supper." Lorna indicated the garden. "It'll be light for ages yet. It's a shame to go in."

Toby ran round the lawn whooping, "Hurray, hurray, hurray!"

Max walked towards her, relief on his face. This was the old Lorna: in the school holidays she and Toby were always making things. Max had often come home from work to find the kitchen table covered in cardboard, newspaper and paint. He used to complain it felt like sitting in her classroom – all they needed were the small chairs.

He grinned. "What's your project?"

"That would be telling, wouldn't it?" Lorna looked at him, daring him to meet her gaze.

He looked away. "Great! I'll get on with supper then."

Lorna and Toby worked in the garden. When she sent

Toby back inside for scissors and sticky tape, Lorna saw Max's shadow jerk away from the kitchen window.

The light was fading by the time she went to tell him they were ready. He was flapping a wet cloth across the stove, mopping up water from the saucepan of pasta boiling over on the ring.

She led him round the side of the house. "Toby, we're coming!"

They emerged onto the empty lawn and stood awkwardly, side by side. The edges of the garden were in darkness now; moths came at them haphazardly, seeking the lit windows.

After a few seconds Max muttered, "Where the hell is he?" Then, "Toby!" he yelled, "Toby! Where are you?"

Out of the bushes a figure ran straight at them. Dark, ragged shapes jostled and floated round it. Max gasped. Lorna screamed delightedly. Toby was naked, his pale skin smeared with dirt. Feathers sprouted from his back and shoulders. More feathers were stuck in his hair.

He circled the lawn twice, flapping his arms. "Crrrrrk! Crrrrrk!"

"Yes! Yes!" Lorna laughed and clapped.

Max stood still. "What – what is this?"

Toby stopped in front of them, panting.

Lorna noticed that all her efforts had not managed to make the feathers – her whole collection – match: Toby had been too fidgety. She hoped Max wouldn't point that out. "What do you think? Do you like it?"

"Like it? What have you done? How – Toby, turn round."

Max steered the child into the light from the porch. Under the layered sticky tape holding the feathers in place, Toby's skin was streaked with blood. Max pulled up a length of tape and the boy cried out. Max examined his son's flesh.

"These are puncture marks." He whipped round. "Lorna! Surely – surely you didn't—"

"It's all right, Dad!" Toby hopped between them, shivering. "It didn't really hurt." His eyes glistened.

Lorna turned on Max. "It was our project! Why do you have to spoil everything?"

"These things are filthy! They're covered in fleas! Stand still, Toby. I'll try not to hurt you." Max ripped off the tape.

Toby winced and squealed, crying now. Feathers fluttered to the ground. Lorna scrabbled to catch them but Max was faster. Crushing the sticky bundles he gathered them up, strode to the back door and stuffed them in the bin.

"Toby, come in and get in the bath. I'll find some antiseptic." Max ushered the boy indoors.

Lorna lifted the lid on the bin. She tried pulling the feathers from the sticky tape but they were ruined.

Lorna slipped out of bed and padded to the window. She pulled back the thin curtains and climbed onto the window sill, the old stone cool beneath her feet. Naked she crouched, knees against her chest, watching the dark slope of the hill. In a few hours the sky would lighten and the buzzards would be back. Through the open window the night air was silky as feathers. She yearned for the feeling of flight. She knew that in another life, an older life, she had been able to soar.

"Lorna!" Max's voice startled her. He draped his dressing gown round her shoulders. "What are you doing? Come back to bed."

"Only two more days!" Max sounded relieved. He was making breakfast for them all in the kitchen. He had insisted Lorna get up to eat with them. Since the incident with the feathers he had kept a close eye on her. He and

15

Toby had stopped going out in the afternoons, too. "It'll be good to get home again, won't it, Tobes?" He slopped scrambled egg onto three plates.

"Yes, Dad."

Lorna knew Toby was only saying what Max wanted to hear. And the thought of going back to the house in the sweltering suburbs, surrounded by bricks and tarmac, made her want to cry.

Max also had other plans. He had told her that she obviously couldn't manage Toby on her own, even if she gave up her job. "We can get some help for you, when we get back," he said. "If it's too much for you," he continued, hitting his stride, "we could look into boarding Toby. Just for one term, see how it goes."

Lorna checked on Toby every night before she went to sleep. Sometimes, waking in the dark, she crept through the silent house to sit on the end of his bed and watch him: his smooth cheek against the pillow, eyelids fluttering in unknowable dreams. The distance between them crushed her heart.

That night it didn't take much to wake him. He smiled sleepily at her. "What is it?"

"Shall we go for a secret walk?" Lorna put her finger to her lips.

She had pulled on jeans and a fleece. Now she helped him do the same. She slid his Spiderman socks onto his warm feet and stuck the Velcro across his new trainers.

She led him down the stairs. The front door key turned easily and they stepped out into the shadowy garden.

The full moon watched them through fingers of cloud.

"Look," she showed him. She wanted him to see everything in her world, all the things Max never saw. They set off up the lane, snails crunching under their feet.

16

"Where are we going?" Toby whispered.

"On an adventure," Lorna said.

"Yes!" He jumped up and down.

"Sssh," she reminded him.

He slipped his hand through hers, and she gripped it like a charm.

There was a stile at the end of the lane. Lorna went over first then helped Toby. Beyond the stile the path rose steeply through bracken, pale and flat-looking in the moonlight. She walked in front. When Toby stumbled on a root, or was surprised by springing leaves, she turned round to him. Each time she looked at him her heart leapt. They climbed in silence. The slope made them breathless.

Near the top, the path led into the windblown trees. Toby asked, "Are we going into the woods?"

"It's not really a wood." Lorna stopped. "We might see an owl. But we have to be quiet."

Her voice sounded far away. Above here the buzzards flew, their streamlined bodies gliding through air.

The thicket was dense, the trees bent almost double by the wind off the sea. The path narrowed and they had to feel their way, ducking under branches that came at them out of the gloom.

Toby cried out: his fleece was caught. Lorna turned back to him and yanked it free. They heard the fabric tear.

"That's my new fleece!" He sounded puzzled.

"We don't have to worry about that!" She went to move on, but he stopped and crouched in the undergrowth.

"I can hear badgers!"

"Badgers don't live up here." Lorna pressed on and Toby followed.

When they came out of the trees the wind was cold and strong. The path ran ahead then turned inland, over another stile. To their left, bracken and gorse sloped away

17

to the cliff edge. Beyond lay the grey sea, waves breaking on black rocks. They stood watching the line of moonlight shiver on the water.

"What are we looking for?" Toby whispered.

Lorna felt the wind's caress, stroking her limbs and tugging at her arms. She took a deep breath, filling her lungs. Her heart pushed at her ribs. Her shoulders throbbed; she glimpsed her daughter's face.

And then, at last, above the wind she heard the child's cry.

"I'm coming." She grasped Toby's hand and stepped off the path.

Toby said something but she couldn't hear. He hung back, pulling on her.

Lorna clamped her hand over his thin fingers, squeezing them. Hot, sweaty fingers, stuck to her skin. She remembered cool skin, pressed against her own; the cold hollow of her empty arms.

"Ow!" Toby leaned away, feet dragging, his hand pushing at hers. "Stop it! No!"

But Lorna was stronger. Gripping his wrist, she started to run.

About the author

Sarah Hegarty was born in Bristol, and has an MA in Creative Writing from Chichester University. Her short fiction has been published in *Mslexia,* the *Momaya Annual Review* and placed in competitions. Two of her short stories were published this year in Spring and Autumn anthologies from Cinnamon Press. Her first novel, *The Ash Zone*, won the 2011 Yeovil Literary Prize. She is one of the mentees on the 2013 Jerwood/ Arvon mentoring scheme, and is working on her second novel. She lives in Guildford with her family.

www.sarahhegarty.co.uk

I Knew It in the Bath

Linda Flynn

(Second in our 2011 Short Story Competition)

Above the steaming taps the spotlight bulb glazes the luminous body of Jessica Snow. Isolated by its beam, she is once again frozen in fear. Her throat constricts, the words are blown away like blossom. She shrugs helplessly, unable to play her part and declares, "I knew it in the bath!"

That cool encompassing womb that encloses all secrets, as safe as a confessional. Within the soothing balmy water her dreams can fly, her confidence can soar.

It's only when she will be forced to emerge, sleek and dripping from the comforting warmth, that she will feel exposed again. Quickly she will flick a towel over her nakedness. Then shivering she will fumble for the soft robe and wrap it tightly.

She feels the sensual anticipation with the clink of the bottle against the cool ceramic. A slight tilt and the creamy liquid splurges in; spluttering against the rush of tap water.

An absent hand swirls the water around, as she longs to cocoon herself in its frothy milkiness. Tentatively she dips her toes, then slowly, sleekly slides in, slipping silkily into a dreamy languor. This is her time, out of time, out of touch, untouched. Except for the thoughts pummelling inside her head, frothing over, then bursting like bubbles. A blink of the eye is like the shutter of a camera, a series of stills. Fragmented memories lie waiting to be pasted together like shattered porcelain. Or thrown, scattered, an urn full of life thrown to the wind.

She lifts a shrimp pink toe out of the water, breaking the line of perfectly formed bubbles. Once again she is

19

dipping her feet into rock pools, sun warmed and mellow. Golden glimmering light ripples the surface, distorting her shell like nails. She throws her head back and smiles, the breeze catching her hair like a careless kite flung behind her. Nearby the thunderous sea spits out its furious spray. Seagulls scream and soar the sky in protest. But she is safe, twirling her toes in a rock pool.

Shouting voices and shrill cries are taken by the wind, lifted higher and higher; sparkling waves of life and laughter. Beach huts turn their paint palette faces towards the sea in a broad beaming grin.

With her arms outstretched she is soaring in waves of wind, wild and free. Her discoveries take her to the Moon's crust, where she poises on one leg in a crater, then dances into the eel like shadows of the sand.

She delights in watching her footprints disappear as she slinks across the gleaming gold. She makes a soggy imprint with one bare foot and watches the sand splurge and suck it down. She lifts her foot out and sees the soft cavity slowly rise and fill, like a sponge cake baking in her mother's oven.

A sturdy red plastic bucket is filled with smooth sand, and then tapped firmly down with a spade. Rubber dinghies bob resiliently upon the churning sea.

There is sand in her sandwiches. But still drunk with her dreams she sips on lemonade and gasps when the bubbles slip up her nose.

With slight fingers she cements her fragile sand castle together with pebbles, sticks and shells. Tottering paper flags flutter in the salty breeze. Purposefully she digs her protective moat, deeper and deeper. Instead of keeping out the invading force of the sea, it seeps in from below, dribbling between her toes and slipping into her clothes like blotting paper.

A sticky hand yanks her back to the shore, away from

the slow sucking shingle and the sliding sorbet sun.

From the promenade she watches her fairy castle, melting like an ice-cream as it slips defenceless, oozing into the sea. The battlements sink in surrender on top of the soggy drowned flags. Greedily the sea runs its tongue over its ramparts, swiftly licking its mound into a memory.

Even the rock pools get swallowed and gorged, their shimmering golden glow submerged beneath the shuddering sea.

A flapping of cotton skirts bid good-bye, alongside a scampering of litter as she dismisses the tossing white spume.

Her fluttering eyelids also sweep good-bye to the childhood rock pools, although she can still hear the incessantly curling waves and the wheeling of the gulls.

Glittering sea spray, swirling water, waves of motion. She twirls the warm water around the bath tub.

The splash, her submersion, their first meeting. They spin, head over heels in a gush of water.

She flies, with arms raised along the water jet; in a rush of exhilaration. Bubbles, laughter and echoing cries resonate around the domed pool.

Screaming she is flung from the tube, cascading into the water with a motion that is not her own. She is unable to catch herself as she is flung across his back. His eyes widen with surprise, as she collapses helpless with laughter.

She slips under water in a blur of voices and veiled vision. She emerges gasping for breath. A steadying arm reaches out and she looks into smiling blue eyes. Around them they hear the distant cries and screams, as shards of light crack the glistening, glassy water. But they are separate and safe, enclosed in their own bubble of time.

She sinks back in the bath with a sigh and raises a

soapy hand to her forehead. A bracelet of bubbles slithers from her wrist.

She sees it all through a miasmic mist, as fragile as a web, as effervescent as a dream. She is a fairy tale princess, wrapped in a lacy haze of veils. Her hair is tucked inside a glittering tiara, away from her flushed pink cheeks. She looks as fragile and lovely as a Wild Rose.

She melts down the aisle in a mist of vanilla spray, which is frothing and foaming at her silk slippers. Her diamonds glint in shards of light. He encloses her hand and circles her finger. The gossamer gauze in her bodice flutters in flight at her breast, but she is ringed.

The moment is captured outside in an endless series of clicks. The heat is stifling. He holds a proud proprietorial arm through hers. In her other hand she tries to balance her heavily wilting bouquet. A cloud of confetti is blown away like blossom.

As she tilts more foam into the bath she remembers the clink of glasses once the champagne has been poured. It spills over the bowls in frothy bubbles of excitement.

She is soaring now, not on the wings of a gull, although they are circling overhead, but on a sleek white yacht. Their honeymoon. Its smooth curved sides slice through the waves, firing exhilarating spume against the deck. The spray shivers in anticipation before slipping back into the sea.

He stands proudly at the helm, controlling the boat's movements as it fights against the rhythm of the sea. He has plotted their course using the best navigational equipment, although they do not venture beyond the perimeter of the harbour.

He pats protectively at the seat which holds the life jackets, encouraging her to sit down. She fidgets, pacing around like a cat. Why can't she be still, even for a moment?

She smiles, acquiescing, but yearning to sit at the bow, with her arms tucked around her legs and her hair flying out like a spinnaker behind her.

At last they slip anchor and tie up next to a bobbing buoy. She pads up onto the roof deck and luxuriously stretches, lapping up the sun. Her eyes close as she is gently rocked by the dipping rhythm of the boat.

He sits up, shocked. She has tried to remove her swimsuit, for all the world to see, to condemn, her brazen nakedness. She shows no remorse, no modesty.

Laughingly she replaces her top, protesting that they are alone in their own watery universe, there is no-one nearby to disturb them. But her words are left helplessly flapping, like the lowered sails.

Below the deep green ocean churns its impenetrable gloom, dappled over with a flickering light.

She submerges into the cabin and he notes with pride its pleasing orderliness. He knows that in a yacht this size everything must be properly stowed away.

She emerges with relief upon the ladder, clinking some glasses together. The cabin smells stuffy and plasticy. In spite of the heat she wraps a robe around her body. It's only her face that she throws to the breeze and the fierce sun.

They had agreed that she would not return to acting. Her career, such as she had, was over. Not in the dimming of the amber lights, but through the interrogative laser beams of the press. He did not remind her of it of course, not directly. But she knew that she had reason to be grateful to him. As for the photographs, well they told their own story.

Yet those were her floaty days, when she seemed to glide through waves of rippling grass. She looked at the world through a shimmery, effervescent bubble. It shut reality out, reflecting it back in a myriad of glistening colours.

The golden glow of summer streaked the fields and

glazed her dark hair with a honey haze. Dizzy with laughter and wine, they stumbled together in a pool of purple clover.

It wasn't that she had not been warned about him; they said that he was dangerous. That was part of his attraction.

She had been shivering on the hillside as the blustery wind flapped her skirt. The filming had taken ages. She was always waiting, waiting, though she had so little time.

The producer sat on the sidelines watching it all, supposedly in the background, but observed by everyone. His black hair was swept back behind him and he had a wry smile on his face. He had the aura of the man who linked all the chains, made the important decisions.

Then soundlessly he had stolen up behind her and firmly encircled a rug around her shoulders. She gave a start and then smiled up at him. It could have been a mink. Later they used that rug again.

It's strange how his presence seemed to invigorate her, whilst others sapped her soul. For people, she often thought were like planets or black holes. Some people had a gravitational pull as they reflected light and energy. Others were more deceptive, hidden black holes that sucked in and destroyed.

But he was bursting with a big, bold light, more like the sun. He exuded a powerful pull of electromagnetic energy and all the other planets revolved around him.

There were some of course who got scorched by him, or who withered in his over powering heat. But now she was standing on the hillside, basking in his light.

The work came pouring in. For she glowed in his warmth and his attention, at last she was noticed, shining in his beam. It seemed as though nothing could touch her as she spun in the pleasure of her own motion, radiating golden sparks like a Catherine Wheel.

24

Then rumours rippled like a breeze across a cornfield. A dark brooding storm crossed his brow and his eyes clouded.

Faces turned away from her, eye contact was no longer held. Contracts started to fall through, her agent became too busy to return her calls.

No longer did she stand in a golden pool of his light. Encroaching shadows crept across and covered her. She shivered in fear as her confidence evaporated.

They condemned her, as only those who truly believe in their own goodness can. The papers carried pictures of his wife and children, gazing out with liquid, admonishing eyes. Slashed to the side she brazenly stood, luridly clad in scarlet. In time she knew that she would read of another who had floundered in his hidden shallows.

Her associates bent together, stooped like poplar trees, with the whispering of their leaves thrown to the breeze.

The greater their secrets, the more they trampled on hers; the more intense their personal misery, the greater their interest in hers.

So she stood like a slender stem in the field, a frothy dandelion clock which had been blown by the wind; slipping away into invisibility.

Hands that have been in hot water too long burn and then they shrivel.

Somehow the moment never seemed right, but she had to tell him, she thought as she plunged her red raw hands back into the washing up bowl. She would choose her time carefully, after dinner perhaps, but before he picked up the evening papers. As long as his mother didn't phone; she so often did on a Friday evening. Just as they were getting comfortable, settling back to watch a film and then they'd hear the imperious ring. He would groan, but leap with alacrity from the sofa. And that would be the end of their evening together.

25

She ground the rough scourer around a saucepan. Or he would go scurrying back to the office. There were so many papers to shuffle. How would she know? How could she possibly understand? Stuck at home, with only domestic duties. She should consider herself lucky. Only someone thoroughly spoilt would complain about leading a life of leisure.

Often he'd heave himself out of his chair complaining of a bad back or his sinuses would be troubling him again. And really if she'd anticipated his needs properly she'd have bought in extra honey and menthol. She could be very inconsiderate.

She bit her lower lip. Sometimes she found it helped if she clenched her fists and dug her nails into her hands.

Of course some evenings he just wanted to get away from her. He needed his leisure, he'd earned it. And as his mother was so fond of telling her, "John does love his sport." Really it's only reasonable to let him have some fun, when he has to work so hard during the day.

How would he greet her news anyway? She'd been careless and really she had no excuse. She stroked her growing roundness, thrilled and frightened by the new life growing inside her.

She rung out her sponge, but it was the dish cloth that she saw in her hands. And even if he did turn away from her for a bit, because after all it hadn't been his decision, he'd get used to the idea eventually. Once he had time to make his plans, then it would be all right. Roughly she dried her hands and shrugged a cardigan around her shoulders.

She pours in a jet of steamy water which whirlpools at her feet. Using her hands as paddles she whirls it around, turning rivulets into ripples, ripples into waves; sucking and surrounding her body in a circling nest.

"Breathe deeply," he urges. "Don't forget to breathe."

26

Stupid advice, for she seems to have no breath, not even to curse. A birthing pool, the right thing to do; so natural, so serene.

The tightening band of pain is merging with the baby's heart. Wave upon wave; deeper and darker in intensity. The pulsing life is eager to escape its rhythmic, warm protective sac. Gradually the grip tightens, bursting into an excruciating crescendo. She gasps and pushes, at first riding the wave, then submerging into it, drowning in a sea of agony. She yells, "Sod the birthing pool; get me an epidural!"

Gasping, sinking. A wave of life comes crashing to the shore. A reverberating scream echoes around the room. Then she holds her pink, helpless baby, his fragile soft skin cushioned against her body.

Her eyes melt at his tiny, tightly clenched fists. A searching little mouth is clinging like a clam, keen to feed. She is swept by a wave of overwhelming love. Their hearts beat in the rhythm of the moment. Keen to keep him safe, she circles him in her protective arms.

She swirls the bath water into rivulets that flow freely through her fingers; scuttling like crabs.

So she returns, like the relentless ocean pounding the shore. Their arms are outstretched, taut with carrying blankets, brollies, laden bags and waterproofs.

Her exposed eyes squint at the watery sun as it slips behind the hazy clouds. Purposefully they stride across the endlessly stretching sands which are miraging into the sea.

He points. They stop. They deposit themselves in the spot, marking their territory.

He checks the sand, the wind direction, the tidal times. You can't be too careful. Out pour the nappy bags, the gritty sun lotion, insect repellent and sun glasses. Safe from the elements they huddle together, enclosed by their wind shield.

Already the bath water has cooled. She leans back against a boulder of frothy bubbles and sighs.

So her mother-in-law makes her weekly visit, punctually at 9.00. There is no need to answer the door, for her mother-in-law has her own key.

Hurriedly she wipes the egg yolk from Tommy's mouth and clears up some splattered food from the floor.

The mother-in-law makes her inspection, taking it all in, the pile of dishes at the sink, papers sprawled across the sofa and toys spilt all over the floor. She blows a floating kiss to Tommy, who will get a hug when he is properly presentable.

But Tommy won't be cleaned and he won't sit quietly. He is fractious as he always is in the presence of her mother-in-law. His face pinks and puckers as the tantrum prepares to erupt. Egg is flung across the floor, the sofa, the lamp shade.

She heaves him out of his highchair and tries to engross his attention in a children's story. For a moment they are together, their heads bent in caring communion. It is a Fairy Story and Tommy likes the pictures. In his excitement he flings the pages open, wildly, at random. And really he should begin backwards, with the girl marrying a handsome prince, only to discover that she's just kissed a frog, then yearning to wake up, to discover that it's just a dream.

Her mother-in-law shuffles impatiently on the sofa, for she can only endure so much indolence. "I don't like to interfere dear, and I'm sure you've got your own way of doing things." This said with a snort, the way a bull widens its nostrils when it is preparing to charge. "But I really do think that you should try to be more organised."

She has left the room, but the odour of her presence remains.

Perched at the side of her bath is a yellow plastic duck with a squashed beak. It can't float very well anymore, not since Tommy bit into its backside.

Later on Tommy rejected it, announcing that ducks are brown, boring sludge brown, not bright yellow.

When is it that we lose our capacity for colour and shape? When does our life become dull and blurred at the edges?

To a child a train is an exciting assortment of shapes in primary colours: red rectangular carriages, round green wheels and a yellow cylindrical funnel. To an adult a train is just a grey blur.

Tommy the commuter now restlessly paces the platform, glancing at his watch to check the time. A drizzly mist falls, blurring the edges and blunting all feelings.

Tommy will weave through the underground, oblivious of the haze of faces. He will scramble through the rush of people, deftly dodging shapes, scurrying into the gap. Like Sisyphus he will perpetually trudge up and down the escalators, heaving his weary form, carrying the shackles of his life, never reaching the top.

In his office pay roll his employees are numbered, their output is carefully calculated. And he will work and work, unrelentingly, until the day comes when he too will lose his productivity.

Uneasily she shifts in the bath, banking up against a wall of bubbles.

She's bending over a box, her face in a veil of tissue. They are moving up in the world, to a bigger house. He has made all of the arrangements, but now she must show less of the slack dreaminess, more purposeful activity. She can't expect him to do all of the work. But really the heat is so suffocating.

Row after row of boxes stand sentry in the hall.

29

Reproachfully the labels lie ready to be stuck in place.

Wearily she lifts a sheet of bubble wrap and winds it around her wrist. She knows that she disappoints the perfectionist in him sometimes.

He covers the hall in a few quick, purposeful strides, glaring at her languor. She opens the flap of a box, staring into the gaping mouth which is waiting to be fed.

He scoffs at her childishness, at all the rubbish that she has gathered over the years; silly trifles, unnecessary tat. Lightly they are covered in a gossamer mist of tissue paper, and then packed side by side. The box is firmly shut; there is a wrenching of brown tape, at last it is sealed, safe from the elements.

His head flicks back and forth at the pretty woman on the television; he smiles adoring her witty comments.

She tears off more wrap to enclose a family photo-graph. There they stood, neatly in a row, poised plasticine people, smiling on command. A click and the moment is kept; Tommy's childhood is encapsulated in a respectable rectangular frame.

She remembers that day clearly; somehow she just couldn't get things together. She was drudge weary from too many sleepless nights. Lunch had been cooked in an abstracted lethargy; the carrots had bubbled over, frothing across the cooker and burning the hob. He sighed.

Then she managed to spill some sauce on to her top and he clicked his tongue impatiently, for now it meant that she would have to change her clothes yet again. Various items were already sprawled across the bed, drooping like limp rags, until finally she had decided on a plain black jumper.

He frowned as she walked down the stairs. He did not criticise her.

She remembers when she too stood in the limelight, not packed away.

Absently she begins bursting the bubble wrap, enjoying the satisfying pop as each globe flattens. He scowls at her drooping shoulders, sagging jowls and grey elasticated waistband.

She holds it inside, breaking a fistful of bubble wrap which bursts the constrained silence in a bitter explosion.

So too, in the bath she kicks against the bubbles, but as one breaks another is formed.

She has escaped. She knows it's wrong. But it's really only a coffee. It is such a long time since they last met and it's not as though they would be alone together. It was quite a coincidence, bumping into him at the station like that. Why shouldn't they want to catch up, to hear each other's news after all this time? And he has been very successful; she had seen his name on plenty of credits. Of course she is going to be a little bit curious. And really, what could be more innocent than a quiet cup of coffee in a café? The guilt seems such a small price to pay for the thrill, the electrical charge which flows right through to her fingertips.

Then there's his intense, unfaltering gaze, flattering and attentive. He will notice the way that she has combed back her hair and the curve of her new red dress. And it's not just him. For suddenly she feels vibrant and attractive again, like a new life is pulsing through her. She tingles with the exhilaration of shedding her old skin.

Hurriedly her heels clatter along the street, following her steaming breath. Her hair is flung out behind her. She turns the collar of her coat up against the cold and she buries her pink nose inside.

At last she scuttles towards the door, gasping in the warmth as she melts inside. Her only greeting is from the boiling urn and the shiny table tops, but still she smiles, her cheeks flushed with a rosy glow of anticipation.

Wedged behind the counter is a round faced assistant, his expression as bland as a coaster. She muffles her order, almost guiltily, before shuffling to a corner and gazing out of the steamy window.

On each table, in a single glass vase stands a pert red carnation. How she hates carnations, with their fake, pointy, papery petals. Her pink fingers wrap like tentacles around the creamy cappuccino. She curls her slender neck towards the frothy, creamy bubbles, as they burst one by one.

He is habitually late as he hates to be kept waiting. And wait she would. Outside the streaming flow of traffic keeps up its heaving flow of movement. Outside the world is chugging and turning. Inside her stomach is churning. But she cannot move. Not until all her bubbles have burst, and perhaps not even then.

As she leans back in her bath she shuts her eyes, shrouding herself in darkness. Luxuriously she stretches out her limbs. The windows are steaming, stark white against the velvety black sky.

Night cloaks their special secret, wrapping it softly around them like sweet summer dew.

Stealthily she steals through the streets of shifting shadows and torrid dreams. Her heart thumps with suppressed ecstasy. She is drawn like the tide, pulled towards his beckoning finger.

She shudders as the screeching of an animal reverberates, shattering the silence. She sighs. Waiting wishing, it flames.

She remembers that moment, just knowing. Swiftly a glance is exchanged between blazing, coal black eyes. Sweet silence, it promises such treasures.

They fly together like ravens, deep and dark. Lips are

32

parted in a smile, a guilty grimace, in silence. They cling together, then let go.

Through the streets as dark as an empty stage set they creep; matching echoing footsteps, blanketed by the balmy night.

Inside his gleaming car their shuddering breaths steam the windows. They burn in the agony and the ecstasy of wanting. Two flickering embers merge into one flame. She's unable to stop, but she knows that it cannot continue. Frantic fingers are fumbling, soothing and stroking. A shadow flickers across the window panes, a sultry silhouette of their dreams and desires. The inky shapes are fluidly forming and spinning in their own motion.

Expelled into the now chill night air, she watches her steaming breath evaporate. The frosty silence is shouting. She knows that there is no beginning, only an ending.

The front door shudders shut. A dark, surly umbrella stares at her with pointing fingers. She hears black recriminations in the reproachful silence. So she buries herself into the deadly, deep impenetrable darkness, screaming inside.

In a glistening sweat she dreams; tossing and turning, feverishly murmuring. She reaches for a shadow that cannot be caught, whimpering as it slides between her fingers. The ebony hair merges with the night, long and glistening and gone.

She lies back, allowing her hair to trail in the bath water like weeds. Ophelia like, she dips under then rises; a crown of bubbles forming around her head. Like a wave, the water breaks over her, engulfing her body. She feels as though she is slipping under a silk coverlet, sliding, melting.

She tries hard to focus her dark eyes on the number disc on his jacket, trying to make sense of the sequence, to find some sort of order to things.

He perches awkwardly and oversized on the edge of her sofa. There is a lady too; she is vaguely aware, making cups of tea in her kitchen. Both present bland, careful faces.

She realises that the police officer is speaking, but his voice seems to come from far away. She recognises the appeal in his tone, the need to find an explanation.

"He had all of the correct safety equipment. His harness was secure; all of his navigational aids were working properly. It was just one of those strange things, a freak accident."

He studies her rock-like immobility. Lowering his voice slightly he leans forward. "There is just one thing that we don't quite understand.," his face is calm, showing studied patience, "Why did he venture out then?"

Why then? He would have followed all of the shipping reports. Why would such a careful, meticulous man decide to sail in force 9 gales when storm warnings were on the national news?

She stares back at their hands clasped in thoughtful, professional concern. Then she closes her eye-lids to present a blank screen. They must not see the flickering images inside her head.

He snaps his book shut. There is a finality, a closing chapter. He will log the paper work, the name, time, date and incident number.

In a wave she sees his doughy face, coated with fine white foam. His bloated, pallid skin is as waxy and lifeless as an extinguished candle.

His ashes are thrown to the swollen grey sea. It crashes into gaping black caverns, spitting venomous spray. Like confetti he is taken up by the blustery wind, hurled up into the ashen sky.

Still the sea continues its heaving pulse of death, its

34

endless pull at the churning shingle.

What chapters of his life would his glazed fish eyes have seen as he stared downwards into the jade water? Which lightning images would have lasered across his mind?

With a flick of her foot she tugs at the plug chain. The water is churned into a groaning black whirlpool. A pale segment of warn away soap is caught in the torrent and plunders into the depth, submerged, drawn under.

Her feet leave damp imprints upon the white tiles, slowly to be sucked into the wraiths of steam, leaving nothing behind.

She shivers, she cannot get warm. Even shrouded in the soft creamy towel her body is as cold as a statue. The last glistening drops of water slip off her alabaster skin and fall.

About the author

Linda Flynn's books *Hate at First Bite* for 7-9 year olds and *My Dad's a Drag* for teenagers have won The Writers' Billboard competition.

She has published with the Heinemann Fiction Project and in Bridge House's *Going Places*, in *Devils, Demons and Were-wolves* and *Hippo-Dee-Doo-Dah*.

She also writes theatre reviews and articles on dogs.

Linda is Head of English and PR at a school in Middlesex. She enjoys swimming, reading, walking her rescue dogs and spends far too much time daydreaming.

Linda's website is: www.lindaflynn.com

Just a Name

Farah Ahamed

Kampala, Uganda

Sunday, February 5th, 2005

12 a.m. I am waiting. I call Marc. No answer.

I flick on the television for the midnight news. The Ugandan government is planning to ban "The Vagina Monologues", a play by Eve Ensler, on the grounds that its title is obscene. The play's organisers, an international NGO, *Akina Mama wa Africa*, try to explain that it is the content, and not the name of the play that matters. The Vagina Monologues were meant to educate and inform the public. The play is based on interviews with hundreds of women who discuss issues such as violence, sexual harassment, rape, incest and domestic battering. *Akina Mama wa Africa* means 'solidarity amongst African women'.

I always show my solidarity. I accept. I conform. I keep silent.

There is much discussion. The Minister of State for Information and Broadcasting thinks that the matter ought to be decided by the Cabinet. There will be meetings with the Office of the President, Churches and other NGOs. Women's rights are taken seriously by the government; Uganda has "gender-friendly" laws. Of course, everyone knows that legally and constitutionally, all Ugandan women are accorded full and equal dignity with men. The Minister says the government is grappling with cultural taboos, erosion of traditional values, modern immorality and the abuse of the rights to freedom of speech through unfavourable art forms. He is in no doubt there is an

36

international conspiracy to corrupt the morality of Ugandans. The ghost of Western values is back again in a new form, to eat away at the moral fabric of Ugandan society. I listen and wonder if we should go and watch the play to show our support, our solidarity. The play is scheduled for February 19th, 2005 at the Ndere Cultural Centre.

5 a.m. Marc has just come home.

Monday, February 6th, 2005

I ask Marc why he slapped me last night. He says he cannot remember. I remind him. I had waited for him all night, and when I asked where he had been, he slapped me. He says he is sorry. He is under a lot of pressure at work. He is working with Lydia on a project. He had not meant to hurt me. I should know that.

Lydia.

I change the topic. I tell him about the fiasco around "The Vagina Monologues" and ask him what he thinks.

"That play was banned in Kuala Lampur, in 2002, because the *public* complained. Here the *government* is complaining, that the play is obscene and pornographic, more so, because it is being presented under the guise of women's liberation. I can't understand why the whole thing has been hyped up so much. It's just ridiculous!"

I keep quiet.

What is ridiculous? The stories about violence against women are obscene and pornographic. Is that what is ridiculous? An occasional slap from a drunken husband who sleeps with other women. These are not forms of violence. It is ridiculous to talk about them. They are commonplace, part of normal, family life. Part of my culture, Ugandan culture. The culture that keeps me quiet.

37

I say nothing.

Marc is home tonight. He receives a phone call at 1.00 a.m. I don't ask who it is. I rub my cheek where he slapped me. There is no scar or bruise. I am not sure if I feel pain. What am I supposed to feel?

Only silence.

Tuesday, February 7th, 2005

The media and pressure groups are fuelling the vagina debate. The public reacts. Hardly anyone has ever heard of the play, but this does not matter as most people know what a vagina is. (It is not a state in America!). There are strong opinions. A radio show host says the play is just a series of monologues about stories of abuse and violence, disrespect and betrayal. These are familiar stories about what happens to ordinary women. What was the huge furore about? He invited people to call in.

One caller responds, "There is no need to make a public display about vaginas. It is immoral and against African culture to talk about such things. To discuss women's lives and bodies in this way is so disrespectful."

Another says, "It should not be allowed. It is a good thing that the government has decided how we should talk about our lives and has told us what words are acceptable for us to use and what words should not be used in public."

I wonder, is the government regulating and banning words? Names?

Another caller is outraged at the government's culturally narrow minded attitude. He argues that the vagina is just a name for a body part. It could have been a kidney or a liver. But the name symbolises female sexuality. That's why the name matters.

38

11.00 p.m. Marc and Lydia have been friends for six months now. He is with her all the time. They have a lot to talk about, but I know it is not just about work. It never has been. Lydia is just a name; she could have been Monica or Sue. Her name doesn't matter. But it does matter, a name matters, doesn't it?

2.36 a.m. Marc just came home. I say nothing to him. I count the minutes he has been away.
The silence continues to tick in my stomach.

Wednesday, February 8th, 2005

Akina Mama, the NGO, say Ensler's play intends to raise awareness of violence against women in a shocking and unique way. They are resolute that the play should be staged, even though the government has criticised it and not all the public, including women, have shown sympathy or support for it. I listen to the debates aired on the radio, devoid of emotion.

What does it matter to me, whether it is staged or not?

The play was banned in China in 2004, because the government said "it did not befit their national situation", and the name of the play and the word "vagina" was uttered too many times throughout the performance. This made them wary and suspicious.

Uganda's situation is not unique. My situation is not unique. I am just like everyone else.

10 p.m. Marc says he will be home soon. I am relieved.

11 p.m. I ask Marc, where is Lydia tonight? I know the answer will leave me dissatisfied, but I cannot help myself.

"Poor Lydia, she is all alone. She has moved to Kampala only recently from New York, as a UNIFEM consultant to the Ministry of Gender. She has no friends. She has nowhere to go after work and lives all alone. She needs company, her family is so far away. This is all overwhelming for her. She is in a new culture".

I wonder if "poor Lydia" understands the "new culture". I could explain it to her. I am completely irritated at myself and at Marc. I don't show it.

Thursday, February 9th, 2005

10 p.m. I watch the late night news. The Minister of State for Information and Broadcasting made a statement to journalists.

"As a country, the corruption of our morals is continuing apace. The corrosive threat posed by individuals who do not care about our society and their Western supporters outside Uganda is one of the greatest challenges of our time."

There is opposition from the Minister of Ethics and Integrity, who says the ban is a move by the government and the Media Council, to silence victims of domestic violence and sexual harassment. Parliament is divided. Public opinion is divided.

Marc and I are divided.

I buy two tickets to the show. The proceeds are going to support the prevention of violence against women in Northern Uganda. I show my solidarity.

4 a.m. Marc comes home; he pushes me away and sleeps on the couch. I imagine Eve Ensler asking me: "If your vagina could speak, what would She say?"

I would say, She has an answer. I have an answer. Her

40

answer is Her Silence. As is mine.

Friday, February 10th, 2005

The Uganda Bureau of Statistics released its latest Demographic and Health Survey. More than 75% of Ugandan women, across all different classes and tribes, accept the culture of violence. I am now just an official statistic.

10 p.m. Marc says he is going out, he will be late, I should not wait for him. I watch him leave.

12 a.m. I call Marc. No answer.

1 a.m. The silence ticks on.

2 a.m. Someone laughingly told me, years ago, "Marc changes his women, just like he changes his shirts." I ignored the comment. What could I have said? I wait, while Marc changes his shirts. I wait. He changes shirts. I wait.

3 a.m. I open Marc's cupboard, and look at his shirts hanging there.
Everyone knows he changes his shirts again and again. Is there such a thing as a passing fling of eleven months? There had been others; the flings had been much shorter. But Lydia is different.
She is not just a name.
Not just a statistic.

Her name matters.
I call Marc. No answer.

4 a.m. I use a small pair of sharp scissors. I snip all of

41

them. Off. First all of those down the front of the shirts. Then those at the cuffs. There are at least two dozen shirts. I hear the buttons clatter to the floor as I snip them.

5 a.m. I pick up them up and put them in a box. They are all round and different colours. Why have I waited years to do this? The shirts are back in the cupboard. The hooks facing the same direction, the crease down each sleeve perfectly ironed.

6 a.m. Marc is home. I did not ask. He did not say.

Saturday, February 11th, 2005

A quiet day. Marc does not say much.

I hear on World News that the BBC is critical of the Ugandan government's ban on the play. It argues that the play should be allowed to be staged because the play was about "Female sexuality and strength".

Female sexuality and strength. I have my own ideas about weakness and strength. Be weak and walk away. In shame.

Nobody does.

Be strong and put up with it. With dignity.

Everyone does.

I am just like everyone else.

Strong.

I do not walk away from a marriage. Or traditional morality. Or cultural values. I know that Marc must love me. He must need me. I know he wants me. I give him stability. I am the one he really loves. That is why he comes back to me, each time. The other women are not important. They are just names. The late nights and rage were just pressure from work. He did not really mean it. I should use my sexuality and strength. To keep him mine.

Sunday, February 12th 2005

Marc wore a t-shirt today. He did not open the cupboard or see the shirts. I wait for him to discover. I regret my anger and my childish reaction, I should have been calmer. I do not have the will or patience to sew the buttons onto the shirts, but I know I must. I must do it soon, before he realises. Marc does not go out and his presence makes me feel powerless.

Tomorrow, I will fix the buttons. I must. I cannot be defeated.

I will repair the shirts.

Female strength.

Tonight, I want him to want me. I try to please him with light conversation, I wear a negligee.

Female sexuality.

Marc stays home all night. Lydia is not important. I am.

Monday, February 13th, 2005

10 p.m. Marc goes out. He wears a sweater. He does not see his shirts. He says he will be home later. At last, my opportunity to fix things. I get out the buttons and I try to sew them on. One by one. I do two more. I can do no more.

1 a.m. I try again. One by one, I am sure I can do them

all. But I cannot.

2 a.m. I look at the box, too many buttons, too many minutes of waiting, too many silences.

3 a.m. Marc is home.
   I pretend to be asleep.

Tuesday, February 14th, 2005

We discuss the morning news at breakfast; the play is now referred to as "The Monologues". The "V" has been dropped. Marc agrees with the Information Minister, the name of the play was intended to corrupt the morals of Ugandans. But what's in a name? Was Lydia just a name? I ask him if he is attracted to Lydia. He is taken aback, looks surprised. Yes, he has to admit, she is attractive. He asks me if I think the play is immoral. I keep silent.
   "African culture and Christian values ought to be protected. It's a good thing the government is doing its best to clamp down on the Western conspiracy and the ghost of immorality".
   I say nothing, but he is right, there is a conspiracy and a ghost. A Ugandan conspiracy to keep the culture of silence.

The ghost had many names; Lydia was one of them.

Wednesday, February 15th, 2005

8 a.m. Breaking News: The government has issued a threat of arrest to Akina Mama if they go ahead and stage the play. The Ugandan public don't know what to make of

it. Some say the banning, and now the threats, are unfair and unconstitutional. Others say Ugandan culture is sacrosanct, it should never be questioned or challenged.

I am uncertain and I feel panic. What have I done? I should not have been so hasty. I should accept my Ugandan marriage. It is this way for everybody. Why should I be different? I go back to the box and try to sew on another button. One by one, I can do this. I can.

I cannot. My fingers don't let me.

10 a.m. Marc found his shirts. He pulls out shirt after shirt, not a single one is intact. I watch him, dreading the anger to come. He does not look at me; I stand near the door and watch him. He turns, I am holding the box of buttons. He snatches and flings it.

"You bitch!"

The buttons clatter to the floor, the sound unusually loud. He pushes me on to the bed, raises his arm, takes a deep breath. Then he turns away. The door slams. I should have sewn on the buttons. I could have tried again, one by one, I could have done them all. It is too late now.

The buttons are scattered.

The shirts are a crumpled heap.

The house is quiet. I don't know what to do. I lie on the bed and wait for Marc.

10 p.m. Twelve hours have elapsed since Marc left.

12 a.m. I call him. No answer.

1 a.m. I see the buttons on the floor, waiting. Waiting to

45

belong to their shirts again. I lie on the floor beside them and wait.

2 a.m. I play with the buttons. What use are they now?

5 a.m. Marc is still not home.

7 a.m. I wake up on the floor. He did not come home. I pick up the buttons one by one.

Thursday, February 16th, 2005

11 a.m. Marc phones me. "Explain yourself," he says curtly. So I tell him. I tell him I only want what all women want. Not anything more. Nothing different. I want him to love me and respect me. Clean shirts in a cupboard, buttons intact. No more changing shirts, no more Lydia.

Marc listens. He says he needs to think things over. I am hopeful. Lydia is just a name.

Maybe.

If Ensler asked me today, "If your vagina could speak, what would She say?"

I would say, She has an answer. I have an answer. I can explain My silence; Her silence.

I have a monologue. It is an ordinary one. I am a hypocrite. I bought tickets to a play to show my solidarity for prevention of violence against other women. I am no different from other women. I keep the silence. My silence is an accomplice to a cultural conspiracy.

But, I broke the silence today.

Friday, February 17th, 2005

Akina Mama wa Africa are interviewed in the newspaper.

They say silence gives way to songs and stories, stories to conversations and conversations to action.

I wonder, does breaking the silence do that?

7 p.m. Marc calls. He says I am asking for the impossible. He could love two women, many Ugandan men did. It is the norm, I should know this. It was culturally acceptable. Why was I being different? Of course, he still loved me, but I had gone too far. He did not want to be with me anymore. I was a difficult woman. He could not take the pressure of living with me, knowing that I was always waiting. He would live with Lydia and visit me, whenever he could. I should not wait. He did not need his things, he was buying new shirts. I do not know what to say. So I keep quiet. He hung up.

It is very quiet. The sounds of waiting used to fill my mind. Now there are none.

Saturday, February 18th 2005

The New Vision has the following headlines: "Ugandan government does not back down; V Monologues are banned!"

The newspapers can't say the name "Vagina".

It's just a name, I scream in my head.

There is a response from *Akina Mama wa Africa* saying they will not stage the play and refund all the money they received for the tickets. They still insist that any act of resistance, no matter how small, matters.

What does it matter?

I listen for an answer.

I hear nothing.

Only silence.

47

About the author

Farah Ahamed is a lawyer and education professional by training. Her short stories tend to reflect on the relationship between the state, society and the individual. Her writing has been published by *Kwani?*, Fringeworks and Fey Publishing

Home

Antonia Chain

This was not the way you had expected the night out to end. The red-orange early morning light breaking through the trees casts a ripple of shadows, spindly and probing across the prone, still figure of the girl who pays no mind to the joyous calling of the birds celebrating the dawn of their new day. A bull terrier, not known for friendliness, pulls its nose forward hard on its lead toward the scrub where you wait to be seen, but its owner, needing soon to be elsewhere, yanks back with an impatient admonishment and the beast reluctantly walks onward down the stone-chipped path. In the distance the low throaty growl of a motorbike rises and falls as a commuter begins his working day, and a siren can be heard, another reminder that life goes on. But you are not reminded and you care for nothing now.

You hadn't wanted to come but a couple of drinks into the evening, the throb of the music catches the primal place within and the dance floor pulls like a magnet, steps heart-gladdening and explosively urgent. A rainbow pulse of lights bounces through the misty miasma above the darkened bobbing, intimately close silhouettes of those elbowing for space. You feel tribal synergy with the shape-shifting crowd. The floor is sticky beneath high stiletto heels that nip and pinch with each step and you notice this but it also makes you strangely happy. The music is everything and everywhere and the heavy bass beat pounds in your chest as the DJ cranks up and the noise rises up through your heels and hits the rhythm of your beating heart. On the periphery of vision you notice the group, dressed in luminous pink and matching t-shirts.

You don't bother to read the slogans which you know will be crowd in-jokes, funny only to that party. The hen wears a veil, plastic tiara skewed lopsidedly over her ear and with every bounce beer from the pint she is holding slops to the floor. Four of the group circle her, arms linked, swaying and in the middle of her coterie she holds her pint high in the air, flabby midriff exposed. The tiara slides further down over her ear. The group do not notice either the expanding void or the glares of those around them beginning to grow weary of the spilt beer and lack of adherence to dance-floor etiquette.

Therese leans towards your ear. She shouts something but you cannot hear. Her arms gesticulate. Still, you do not understand. She too is wearing a t-shirt. Her logo, in silver on black says 'Angela's Army' as does yours. You didn't think it was a good logo and you didn't want to wear a t-shirt, or pay ten pounds for the privilege but the night on the town to celebrate Angela's forthcoming nuptials took on a life of its own, planning military in precision and you wonder if anyone, even Angela, is actually enjoying it. The curry was nice enough but sorting the bill a nightmare and you resented paying for all the brandy and cokes since you were pacing yourself with spritzers. The wine bar was cool though the drinks were expensive but at least the hens managed to intimidate a group of boys out the corner and colonise the seats. You were relieved and hoped to spend the rest of night there seated, off the heels which had looked great in the wardrobe mirror but were less great walking endlessly round town.

You were glad the night was drawing to an end and, having showed willing you could reasonably leave, no feelings hurt, no unwritten rules of office based friendships breached. But then a move to another club was suggested. "We are going to The Harly" Therese shouts pointing towards the door in an exaggerated theatrical mime. "Come on". Angela and others in the party swarm by the door. Angela's make up looks gothic. She has been crying. Gina has managed to rid herself of the hideous t-shirt. Why hadn't you thought to wear something under yours? You wish you had also remembered to wear flatter shoes because your feet, already feeling as if they had stepped on pins now have to walk the half-mile to the next club. You do not want to go and you imagine that the looks on the other girls' faces suggest that most feel the same. Discussion and debate however, is not a possibility in the noise and so, reluctantly, you follow Angela's Army down the stairs and into the thronged street awash with revellers paused between places to be. You notice Somoya peeling off from the group and imagine you see her shoulders lift as if free of a burden. You have never met her before but feel sympathy for her. She didn't drink and judging by her forced smile tonight has been more of an ordeal for her than for you. You are envious when she escapes and wonder if some of the other hen's comments as they gaggle together discussing her early departure border on racist.

Your feet hurt badly and you really do not want to go to the Harly though it is one of your favourite nightclubs where the music is unashamed disco. Off the beaten track and frequented by those in the know who, like you, enjoy the camp décor and anything goes clientele. Angela and her gang are going to sight-see and understanding this fills you with dread. Your suggestion of a different club causes sneers and the vaguest of hints that you are – at best – unadventurous and at worst maybe a little bit homophobic. You do not respond because 'my best friend is gay' is to your mind, one of the most homophobic things straight

51

people say. So, you hobble in your too high heels and feel secretly a little bit pleased when the Harly doorman recognises you.

"Oooer, are you a little bit that way then" says one of Angela's Army, theatrically bending her wrist using a gesture so beloved of bad TV comedy shows.

You cringe and offer an apologetic look to the door-man but he looks back, less friendly and waves you all in.

The flock descend on the bar and the purse-holder asks for yet another tenner from everyone. You certainly hadn't drunk thirty pounds worth in the last club so you feel a bit ripped off but know it will be seen as churlish to raise it. It is the only tenner left in your purse. The walk home will be long tonight.

Your hen night will be simple and small, you think – if you even bother to have one. Marriage is not something yet discussed but thinking about it makes you feel happy and worry about the walk home fades. You will be glad to get back to Oliver.

The ranks of Angela's Army vie for floor space with the other hen party seen at the previous club. They too had decided that a gay club was the perfect venue for straight women on the town. You prop yourself against a rail watching the pulsing crowd, resting one foot at a time. An elbow gives a deliberate nudge to yours. He returns your glance left with a nod and a raise of his pint. You smile neutrally and give a slight nod back and return to watching the hens compete dance with each other. Then, the nudge again. He mimes a graceless shimmy with a point to the dance-floor and you notice his ruby red earring catch the disco light as you mime back no thanks. He leans in, his mouth close to your ear and out of a reflex memory of politeness you lean forward to hear him. "Ugly fat bitch" he says. Sour, tobacco smelling spittle sprays onto your cheek. You are not upset so much as disappointed.

The dance-off between the hen parties takes on a different aura. The previous bonhomie with an edge has become less bonhomie and more edge. The inevitable drink fuelled shove arrives and soon leads to a half-hearted girl fight with fake hair pulled and slaps exchanged. You see the doormen wade into the fray and without stopping to ask who or why they peel the fighting women from each other and march them to the door. The women on both sides follow protesting the innocence of their particular hen but no one is listening and the void in the dance-floor is liquidly filled. Across the floor you see earring man glare at you, paying no attention to the arguing hens. You decide to wait a while before you leave. "What on earth happened" you will say in the office on Monday. "I went to the loo and when I came back everyone had gone".

It's funny how things turn out. You start at Sawden's and within the first week Angela, showing you the office ropes, quickly morphs into a friend. She is such a laugh! You envy her a little bit because she is pretty in a dark, mischievous way. You once read about a film actress being 'smouldering' and this describes Angie. She is the office flirt but it is all good-natured. You were glad to gain office popularity just by virtue of being her friend, and later flat mate. When she met Mike – her husband-to-be – you gossiped together about her luck and once upon a time, rather than being a reluctant add-on invite to the hen party you would have been the chief bridesmaid or perhaps second bridesmaid after Angie's sister. Neither of you ever mention the seismic shifts in your friendship which begins when Oliver starts working in your department. You both giggle over coffee about how completely gorgeous he is. You tease Angie that she shouldn't be looking – what would Mike say? "No harm in looking." she responds, "I'll have that one!"

Only, it turned out, it wasn't Angie he was interested in.

Oliver helps you fix your TV to the wall in the new flat. Even in the stress of the move you enjoy seeing him wield the screwdriver. You both take childlike delight in setting up your first shared home together. Neither of you know what is in half the boxes that litter the floor.

"The most important things are to find the kettle and set the bed up" he says smiling and you are glad to be away from the atmosphere in the old flat and Angela's frozen glare as you and Oliver carried boxes out. She didn't offer to help and you both knew that the bad back explanation was untrue.

The stainless steel rail fencing the dance-floor feels cool against your arms and you lean upon it and try to take some weight off your aching feet. There are few chairs and all of them are occupied or marked territorially with coats. The numbing effect of the alcohol is wearing off and the pinching pain is constant. Still, you enjoy the atmosphere and sway to the music at one with the happy bobbing crowd. Two beautiful young men sway close together, sex clearly on their minds, oblivious to the fast disco beat all others on the floor dance to. The track changes and as a mass the crowd jump to the air, arms raised and swaying and there is joyful abandon in the atmosphere. You catch the sickly smell of the saliva on your cheek and realise that ear-ring man stands close to you. He returns your glance. His eyes are unfriendly. As you slide along the rail away from him you don't understand why you feel apologetic.

The night air is crisp and the stars have a story-book twinkle in the blue black sky. You are pleased that the doorman is once again friendly as he wishes you good night. A plastic tiara sits in the gutter outside the club. You pull the strap of your bag onto your shoulder and cross your arms over your breasts in an attempt to shield your coatless body from the chill breeze and begin the long walk home. You recall that you never had another drink out of the last tenner you handed over to the hen night purse holder. Although the club is off the beaten track you do not feel afraid as you pass its nearest semi-industrial estate neighbours. The lights are still on in the 'Tile warehouse' showroom and illuminate the road whilst the gates of the recycling centre are locked so that they provide no shadowed hiding place. A few people linger about. "Goodnight darling" shouts an unembarrassed man peeing against a giant wheeled bin as you walk by. Every once in a while, a taxi passes by but it never occurs to you to flag one down though there is shopping cash at home in the tin in the kitchen. Oliver suggested the tin. He said you should both chip in and use it for the main weekly shop and also for the daily lunch money. If there is anything left over at the end of the week, you have a weekend takea-way. It was such a great idea, typical of Oliver. You are looking forward to a chow mein and bottle of wine with him on Sunday night.

The annual all-staff development day is universally disliked. Everyone endures it whilst none of the office staff understand who actually thinks it is a good idea or what it is supposed to achieve. This year the theme is the Olympics. Each table laid out in the conference centre main hall represents a country and each country has a series of tasks to perform. Your table, a collection of people from accounts, office services and HR teams are unified in their understanding that they are rubbish at making a model of a suspension bridge out of paper cups, card and sticky tape. Some of the group fairly soon lose interest but Oliver is determined and pokes his tongue out in concentration as he tries to make the bridge stand up. You think he looks sweet. He sees you looking at him and grins broadly and both of you share an unspoken moment of awkward shyness. The event facilitator walks round the tables, mic in hand, ebulliently congratulating the team for their awesome effort and handing out toffees as prizes. Denny from accounts adds a label 'the bridge to no-where' and although it is not especially funny the whole table begins to giggle until the giggling takes on a life of its own and everyone is almost choking with laughter. Mr ebullient is clearly a bit put out but his efforts to make your team share the joke with everyone else just provokes more helpless laughter. Oliver has his arm over your shoulders as your team rock together in stifled mirth. You see Angie on Senegal's table look over and you know immediately that you have done something wrong but you are not sure what it is. At lunch, Oliver says that in his experience balancing a plate, drink and eating whilst standing is not a skill many people have and that you should share a plate to make it easier. Angie joins you briefly but is frosty and monosyllabic and you are glad when she leaves you and Oliver to your plate of chicken skewers. At the end of the team day someone suggests that you all go to a champagne bar and you drink too many glasses. The date becomes yours and Oliver's 'shagaver-sary', as you call it, but you don't want to tell Angie on Monday back at work because you know she will be unhappy about it. She is. She doesn't say that of course, what she says is "having an affair with the boss is never a good idea" and you wonder why she calls it an affair.

The addictions treatment centre is not open but during the day-time it is a hangout best avoided and instinctively you cross the road though none of the usual dealers hang around outside tonight. Memories from childhood make you look to the left and the right although your hearing has already told you that the road is free of traffic. The crisp air is quiet and still. A figure is walking a hundred feet behind you and you see the sharp glint of the earring catch the streetlight. He knows you have seen him.

The graceful elegant walk of early evening has been replaced by the limping, leaning gait of a girl in heels too high at the end of a long night out. You feel the obvious signs of your pain as a kind of failure and do not want it to be observed by others, but you are not sure why and make more of an effort to walk confidently upright. Your feet burn and the effort makes your back hurt too.

It was so funny when you said to Oliver "I can hardly walk in them," and he said with that sexy look of his that they were the kind of shoes that made people walk to you. He called you 'milady' and you both laughed as he bought them for you. You went for lunch in MacDonalds after and you couldn't remember ever being happier.

The pungent smell of chip grease from the all night café drifts in the air and a throng of lively post-clubbers queue for their burgers. For a moment you are tempted and wonder if there are enough coins left in your purse but know that you will regret it in the morning and so you walk on by. Oliver is waiting for you at home. He will be sleeping and you will slide under the plump new duvet next to him. He will lay his arm around your waist and you will coil together still fresh with curiosity for the shape of each other, even in sleep. You will inhale his ambergris maleness and drift into a contented sleep.

Despite the chill in the air you love the crispness of the early hours of the morning. The sky looks blacker, the stars look brighter and the absence of traffic on roads is a strange delight. The tarmac of the pavement is bumpy and cracked where thick tree roots rebel against containment and your shoes make the terrain hostile. You decide, reluctantly, that the shoes have to be taken off. Walking home barefoot is not an ideal choice but the balls of your feet are burning with pain and all effort at grace is gone from your steps. A rough trunked oak provides a prop and you reach to slide one foot from a shoe. The heel strap is gently peeled from a burst blister. A dog fox appears right in front of you and you freeze. He is magnificent and without fear. This is his night-time domain and you are in it. You stare at him awed by his regal beauty and he stares right back. A moment later, curiosity satisfied, he daintily steps over a garden wall and disappears into the shadows of a hydrangea. He had been close enough to touch and you were stunned by the magic. "Did you see that?" you wanted to exclaim and looked around for others to share the moment with but all you saw was the man with the earring, not walking, but leaning against a wall as if waiting for you to walk on. He is smoking a cigarette.

The shops thin to houses all asleep behind tidy front gardens. In the near distance there is an all-night garage and you think maybe you will stop and browse the shelves for a while though there is little money in your purse. You imagine the floor tiles will be cool on your aching feet. Footsteps behind you sound too close and the garage seem a long way away.

When you took them into work to show her, Angela said she hated the shoes. She said they were prostitute shoes and only a pimp would buy them for a woman. You know she noticed that you have them on tonight.

The museum is one of your favourite places. An anachronism in so many ways: out of the town centre and full of assorted junk that the real town museum doesn't want. It is funded by a private trust dedicated to 'providing educating opportunity for the working man' and the trust cannot be used for any purpose other than the museum. It will be there until the money runs out when the building can be sold and turned into flats. You wonder whether Oliver has ever been inside. By day, the Victorian gothic is elegant alongside the post war utilitarian houses, and you visit it, every now and again though you cannot remember when the last time was. As you walk home, barefoot, in torn tights you find its gothic dark and intimidating and you cross the road noticing that he is there still, a hundred paces away. You tell yourself he probably just lives along here.

The shriek of a girl cuts the chill air and you see a group of people turn into the road and make their way up the street in your direction. Ordinarily you might feel wary but tonight you feel relieved. They look like students, young, slightly scruffy and alternative sorts, the odd tatty dreadlock and stripy jumper. They josh and play fight and make way, opening clam like to allow you to walk through. You smile at them though they do not really notice you. Momentarily you consider asking if you can walk with them, though they are going in the wrong direction. You hasten a glance back but you cannot see earring man and an acre of tension lifts from your shoulders. You are glad you didn't say anything to the students. When you get to the garage, you see that the shop is closed and only the all-nigh hatch is still open so you do not linger.

The straps of your shoes cut into your fingers and your feet really hurt. Your bag slides off your shoulder in the transfer of shoes from one hand to the other and you drop it scattering your purse, lipstick, emergency tampons and phone to the floor. The last of your coins fall out of the purse. As you bend to retrieve the items your knee is punctured by a small piece of glass on the pavement. The gasp is more in shock more than pain and you stand quickly, as your belongings again slip from your hands and into the gutter. You smell cigarette smoke and see him stood, watching, just across the road from where you stand. You brush the blood from your knee and feel tears stinging your eyes. You retrieve your lipstick but leave everything else and hasten quickly towards home.

You wonder if Oliver might still be up and then re-member that he has a football match tomorrow. You love making his kit all clean and nice-smelling packed ready in his sports bag. You play at husbands and wives and it makes you laugh. Oliver would never expect you to have his gear ready any more than you need him to sort the oil out in the car but it's just the novelty of it all and you enjoy the ribbing of your mates about turning into Mr and Mrs Cozy. Oliver will be sound asleep and you imagine getting home and finding that he has probably forgotten to turn the coffee machine off.

Houses with darkened windows and long drives border the silent tree-lined avenue. Somewhere an owl calls. You think it is an owl but realise that you do not really know what an owl sounds like. Does Oliver know what an owl sounds like? The distant hoot prompts a partly remem-bered rhyme which you breathlessly speak out loud into the silence of the night. You remember only the first two lines which you repeat over and over and over and over as you throw your shoes into a garden and quicken your pace. Your two-line mantra drowns out the footsteps you can feel closing behind you.

You will tell Oliver about this awful night. About Angie and her dreadful friends and the fight in the club and money laid out for drinks never had. And you will tell him about the horrible walk home and throwing away the shoes he bought you and the amazing fox and the creepy smelly man with the earring and he will stroke your hair and say you need to be with him so he can take care of you. You will cuddle up to him, enjoying the firm strength of his arms around you and the sweet man smell of him and you won't mind when he doesn't turn the coffee machine off or put his football kit in the wash basket.

You run. Your bare feet have lost any sense of direction or home and do not feel the shards of gravel and stone cutting and embedding into their soles. A den of garden shrubbery unlit by the orange glow of streetlamps suggests a refuge and as you scramble inside thorned branches scratch and peck at your skin. In the darkness, curled small, you try to still the rasping sounds of tortured lungs and chatter of teeth but a rodent screeches an alarm that its domain has been trespassed and you cry out in response. You smell cigarette smoke and hope that someone will find your shoes.

About the author

Antonia is new to fiction writing following a long career wielding a pen in academic environments where she has recently completed her doctorate. She currently lives in Brighton with her partner, and two beloved dogs, and has recently completed her first novel.

Whiteout

Jeanne Davies

THE YEAR 2022

She sat hunched in the corner of the disused warehouse. The world had suddenly become very thin. A draught blew through the broken windows, tossing old bits of newspaper helter-skelter like damaged birds. She knew they'd come and take her soon, but she just had to stop running.

A YEAR LATER...

Mark surfaced from another restless night in a sleepless trance. He wiped his hand across his damp forehead, recalling the visions of stars falling one-by-one from the night sky and then the absolute darkness. A feeling of emptiness choked him and again he was engulfed in a void which drew all life into its nothingness. It was dawn and the curtains bulged in like lungs through the open windows.

A small thread of courage emerged from his hopelessness. He dressed, begrudging the effort; the image in the mirror was of a sepia stranger. He no longer felt hunger but forced down a caffeine drink before taking the lift to the garage beneath the apartment block.

The car locks yielded and he slid his wilting body into the driver's seat. Dragging a deep breath, he set his route. "Your estimated time of arrival is 10.45 a.m." confirmed the automated voice. The garage doors responded to the car's control panel and he sat back and closed his eyes as the car sped away.

Above the soundless engine, there was a groan in the

pit of his stomach. He fought against the nausea which swept over him... which prevented him from finding any peace.

"Activate manual control," he said, pulling the steering wheel from the dashboard cavity.

"Manual controls activated. Your time of arrival is now indeterminate," the voice responded.

The coast road from Brighton was empty, so he turned up the music and put his foot hard down on the accelerator, embracing the adrenalin rush against his numbness. A light drizzle had started and the breeze blew a confetti of blossoms across the road. "I was going to marry her," he murmured, pressing his foot down further. She hadn't believed him; she said he didn't know what love was. For him that had changed, the time she took him to the cliffs above the Marina...

On the day his father died, Becky had driven them out of the university campus towards the coast. Mark watched nonchalantly as the countryside unrolled in layers of green. They parked in the Cliffside car park and climbed the steep winding path to the summit. The wind rushed past, playing drum symphonies in his ears. Walking up to the edge where the land disappeared into the sea, his palms became clammy. As he looked to the distant horizon, he felt he was flying.

"Where did you find this place?" he asked.

"Oh, I used to come here all the time with my friends from school... when we could manage to escape, that is."

"Now why would a nice girl like you want to escape from a prestigious place like St. Michaels?" he teased.

She paused. "You can inhale God here," she said,

63

turning to face him, her silk blouse forming wings of gossamer in the wind. Her hair spiralled from her head, transforming her into an angelic Medusa.

He gazed into her cornflower eyes, which he knew he would compare all summer skies to for the rest of his life. Inside he was dancing. He noticed her pupils expanding and he longed to kiss her, but somehow his teeth got stuck to the sides of his mouth. Instead he stooped down and snatched the largest Marguerite daisy he could find and placed it to her lips.

"That's beautiful," she said. "I've got one of those flower presses somewhere."

Simultaneously they glanced upwards, straining to see a lark fluttering and singing so high it was barely visible against the marbled sky.

"Oh, I nearly forgot... I've something else to show you," she smiled.

She led them to a door, overgrown with creepers and surrounded by long grasses and wild flowers.

"It was opened in 1910 and used as an air-raid shelter in the Second World War. The school used it as its own private access to the beach; it's a good place to hide when you're in trouble."

"This is awesome," he said, rattling the locked gate.

"It's only opened on special occasions, but if you know where to look..." she said, carefully edging her way alongside the concrete structure.

She disappeared, leaving Mark with the wind howling through the gate, like a lonely phantom. She suddenly reappeared looking dishevelled, with pieces of grass poking from her hair. As she held up a key, a huge grin raised her cheek bones to dizzy heights and her eyes gleamed with innocence. He knew he loved her then and always would.

She wriggled the key in the lock and he heaved aside the door. She gripped his hand as they made their way along a dark tunnel, breathing in the escalating smell of the sea. Giggling like children, they headed towards a small dot of light as it grew bigger and then, as if by magic, they appeared on the side of the cliff face.

"Breathtaking," he sighed, sliding his arm around her waist. He drew in her fragrance above the salt.

It was only a short walk down a narrow path to a vast empty beach. Laughing, they chased each other like mud skips until they were spent and too tired to go on. They lay down beside each other on the damp sand, looking up at the seagulls; their plaintive cries telling stories of the vastness and cruelty of the ocean. They shared memories of their diverse childhoods, of their dreams and aspirations. They were so different, but from that day onwards he believed they would be the same person, in body, mind, and spirit; their thoughts would be linked together. As the sun slipped swiftly down under the horizon, they made love and spoke promises only they could ever know. Dusk settled as a cloak over them and, one by one, the stars ignited and rose up into the velvet darkness. He watched her sleeping and captured moonbeams in his hands and spread them over her. She opened her eyes and smiled at him. "Have you got the key?"

"Well, I bloody well hope so, or we'll have to mountaineer those rocks to get back!"

"Or swim... or go to sea in a beautiful pea-green boat!" She chuckled.

He could see her glowing beside him in the tunnel on the way back up. Words were needless; nothing could break the magical silence. They emerged from the gate like fireflies, sparkling in the moonlight. He wanted to hide the key in a different place, just for fun, but she wouldn't hear of it.

"Well, I know one thing, I'm not going to end up like my dad," he said, as they reached her car in the deserted car park. "After mum died, he did everything to get me to Law school and took nothing for himself. He ended up penniless in a revolting care home."

She caressed the back of his head and wiped a tear tenderly from his cheek with her fingertip. "But he had you," she said.

"You have reached your destination," shook him from his day dream. He pulled into the side of the road and switched off the engine. Swallowing hard, he allowed himself to sink into the motionlessness.

The small village of Ford looked like any other rural community these days; a few scattered houses and a village shop which had been boarded up. Everything was delivered directly into people's homes these days, thanks to EITS. Mark's father had warned him about the "Eyes-in-the-sky" from the early days. He had seen it creep in like a cancer through ordinary people's homes as entertainment, internet and telecommunications. It monitored what people watched, what they wanted to eat or to wear; it found out what was important to them. It linked worldwide with payment cards and eventually people were fed with what EITS thought they needed, or wanted... it was all so easy. Mark wondered if anyone else had noticed, or whether anybody really cared. Mark's dad really cared; he'd been a political activist, a man who stood up for the underdog.

Mark checked his pockets and restarted the engine, turning in where a sign said "Ford Prison". Immediately ahead the car faced an arched access and, as he approached, a scanner swiped across his number plate. A screen drew back, allowing his headlights to illuminate a tunnel. The car was propelled ahead on a track and, as it travelled downwards, background lighting switched on and signs indicated Level 1, then Level II and finally Level III, where it stopped at a barrier.

A robotic voice said: "Good morning, Mr McKenzie, how are you today?"

Mark lowered his window. "How I feel is of no importance," he growled. "I've come to see Archibald Scrivener."

"Dr Scrivener is expecting you. Please spread your right hand over the blue pad, and hold for ten seconds."

Mark felt his hand sink into a soft moulding material.

"Ten, nine, eight, seven, six, five, four, three, two, one... please remove your hand now, sir."

The barrier lifted. Mark cruised into a parking space and switched off the engine, allowing the steering wheel to vanish into the dashboard. Automatically, the doors lifted like wings and he unfurled his frail body into a vertical stance. He was suddenly aware of a figure standing by him.

"Good morning, Mr McKenzie, so nice of you to come. You're just in time to watch our first procedure of the day."

"Oh, great," Mark replied with a nervous smile. Both men locked in a firm handshake.

"I always appreciate having interest from defence lawyers... so many of your 'failures' end up in here," Scrivener grinned. "Please, follow me."

They walked in silence, their footsteps echoing like hooves down a long draughty corridor. Scrivener was much taller than Mark had remembered and he had the stance of a much younger man. They reached a huge metal-clad door marked "Whiteout Unit".

"Why did you call it Whiteout?" Mark asked, watching Scrivener's right hand disappearing into a box, which illuminated. The doors ahead opened and the doctor motioned him forward.

"Initially we called it "Wipe-out", but we didn't want to give anyone the wrong idea," he said with a snarl. They headed towards another set of doors which led them into a clinical area, resembling a huge plastic bubble.

A body lay motionless on a table, clad in a white gown; from the size of the body it appeared to be male. The doctor began washing his hands whilst a nurse tied a green apron around him. She tossed a white coat at Mark who stood hesitantly by the door, "You'll have to gown up," she snapped.

"The basis of this serum is a toxic protein which contains two pulsing isotopes," Scrivener said, thrusting his hands into green latex gloves. "The first is designed to seek out the aggressive regions in the brain and to pacify them. The second attaches itself to the pituitary gland to eliminate all sexual desire and make the patient impotent."

"That's clever," Mark nodded. "Is it painful?"

"Well, come closer, I'd like you to judge that for yourself, Mr McKenzie," he said with a confident smile.

The nurse reappeared holding a Petri dish filled with pink liquid which she proceeded to smear over the patient's left temple with a cotton wad.

"Is the patient already anaesthetised?" Mark asked, noticing a lack of response.

"No, only a mild sedative has been administered. This solution acts as a further numbing process and also

68

prevents the possibility of any infection."

He unloaded a small syringe slowly into the patient's temple. Mark held his breath... it seemed to take an eternity. A vein in the head began to bulge and to illuminate. As the liquid travelled, other veins began to light up to form a blue pattern, like a tattoo, across the left side of the cranium.

"As you can see, there is no evidence of discomfort during this process," Scrivener said as he withdrew the needle.

Mark watched as an array of sparking lights snaked throughout the skull, but the body remained motionless.

"And that is it, Mr McKenzie... simple and effective and the inmate will be up and about in approximately twenty minutes from now."

"What about all those lights buzzing in the head?"

"Don't worry, they are merely electrical impulses which will die down very shortly."

"Fascinating; I had no idea it would be that straightforward. Have any of these procedures ever gone wrong?"

"Occasionally there are small complications; for example, an inmate may be pregnant and the procedure will trigger a spontaneous miscarriage. Those cases are taken to theatre and the female is immediately sterilised."

He couldn't bear to think about that. The thought was devastating.

"How can you be sure that Whiteout is totally reversible?" he croaked.

"The isotopes can be retrieved easily with the administration of an antidote, which is injected in exactly the same way. The solution attaches itself to the pulsing micro-silicones left by Whiteout and then passes them out of the body through natural wastage."

"How long would that take?" he asked mechanically.

"That process could be completed within just a day or two," he paused as his face developed into a grin. "The length of time would, of course, depend on the patient's constitution!"

Mark didn't get the joke. He stood frozen, watching the nurse cleaning up and Scrivener removing his protective clothing. The patient remained motionless. He thought of her... what they'd put her through.

"Does the blue tattoo effect remain across the head like that?"

"Not for long," Scrivener said, slicking his grey hair back through his fingers. "After a week or so, a silvery white scar develops in those capillaries. Now... please do join me for some refreshments," he said, gesturing towards the exit.

A tray of coffee had been laid in a long and narrow lounge area, with windows stretching floor to ceiling along one wall. As Mark brought his cup over with him, he realised they were one-way mirrors.

"That group of inmates are being taken to the activity area just prior to visiting the canteen for lunch," Scrivener said, as he approached the windows and eagerly downed his espresso.

Mark watched them shuffling past, like cattle going to slaughter. Their eyes were blank to everything around them as they ambled along, focused on staying in the line. Some of them were nodding rhythmically as they walked and others were hampered by spasms which shook their bodies.

Mark's eyes were drawn like magnets to inmate 273. His gaze settled upon her familiar frame, still slender and beautiful, even with her head shaved. He was in awe of her; but there was something in her stance that was clumsy now. She lacked the grace he'd always loved so much; she held her head in an unnatural way and it scared him. He hadn't been prepared for this.

"Can these patients still talk?"

"We don't refer to them as patients here, Mr McKenzie... after all, they are criminals and this is still a prison."

Mark had to control a sudden urge to swipe him around the head. He took a deep breath. As she turned, he saw the white pattern of scars on Becky's temple and something inside him shattered. His mouth gaped open as he struggled to restrain that inaudible scream.

"Fascinating," he said, swallowing hard.

"Their intelligence has essentially been removed and they are now functioning on a basic animal level," said Scrivener, pointing to a patient licking himself like a dog. "It completely eliminates the need for Wardens here."

"Do they recognise people... I mean those around them who take care of them?"

"As you can see from this group, they barely make eye contact with each other and any significant interaction has not so far been recorded." He sat in an armchair and began sipping his second cup of coffee. "In fact, they are so reluctant to communicate that we find it necessary to give them a complete physical examination once a month to monitor any basic health issues. Of course they are also hosed down on a daily basis for hygiene reasons... the Whiteout procedure seems to completely remove their sense of smell!"

Mark dragged his gaze away from Becky; his heart pounding so fast it almost leapt from his ribcage through his mouth. He wanted to take her now. He could smash the glass and grab her, killing everyone there, just to get her out of this place. But he knew that would be wrong... it was not part of his plan.

"Just out of interest, how many patients have been

71

given the antidote so far?" he asked, taking a notebook and pen from his pocket.

"Well, thanks to the efficiency of prosecution lawyers, we have never had the need to use it. The antidote is kept in a secret Government vault, which even I have no information about." He paused. "What are your plans for the remainder of the day, Mr McKenzie?"

Mark was running over exactly what his plan was now.

"I thought you could take a tour of our young offenders unit which is situated in the traditional part of the prison. We show what the future could hold for these adolescents by involving them in the care of Whiteout inmates on a personal level. It scares the hell out of them. What do you think, Mr McKenzie?"

"Oh, please... call me Mark," he replied, trying to extract his gaze from her. "I would like to learn as much as possible but, at the risk of sounding rude, would you mind if I take a brief walk outside first?"

The doctor looked puzzled but Mark held up a hand-rolled cigarette. "I just can't manage to give up these little buggers."

"I presume you are on the smokers' register?"

"No chance of getting out of that one... EITS knows all about my bad habits," Mark smiled. "I'm proud to say my addiction is clearly recorded on my identity profile and I don't expect to get any medical treatment when it finally finishes me off."

"Well that is very magnanimous of you, Mr McKenzie. Just follow the corridor to your left and go down two flights of stairs; there is a small garden where you should go unnoticed."

Mark found some small release in running. He arrived at some French windows and burst out, inhaling deeply.

He walked across the lawn in the compound area and levered himself like a pole-vaulter over the fence into a field of wild grasses.

"The bloody bastards," he rasped, as he bit down hard on the roll-up paper and began shredding the tobacco through his teeth. "The evil fucking bastards… they have no right to take away people's souls!"

The spring weather was changing and dark clouds loomed like phantoms across the skyline. They hung so low he wanted to reach up and punch them. In the distance was a church spire, sitting like a dunce's hat in the corner.

"You can't keep God locked up in there, you pious bastards," he cried out.

Mark thought back to the day he'd persuaded Becky to come with him to search for secret papers at Scrivener's mansion house; he'd always suspected there was no antidote. She'd been so reluctant to take the pistol but obediently stood outside the study to keep watch, whilst he rummaged through drawers. Something disturbed the housekeeper and then all hell broke loose. The housekeeper's small dog flew at Becky and suddenly the gun fired. He'd wiped her finger prints off and told her to run; he didn't even have time to kiss her. He took a chance that one of them wouldn't come back, but he didn't expect it to be her… the girl of happy endings. She'd been alone and on the run, with police helicopters searching for her.

Mark re-entered the Whiteout lounge, the Nicotine still buzzing in his brain. "I thought you should know that I sent your papers to all the tabloids on my way here this morning."

"You mean the documents you stole from my home?" Scrivener said, calmly placing his coffee cup back on the table.

"The public have a right to know that the antidote is

useless, if it even exists at all!"

"Well, those findings merely said there was no point in using the antidote. But of course you and I know it was merely a fabrication to appease the conscience of the masses."

Scrivener slowly rose to his feet. "Did you really think that I wouldn't piece together your connection with Rebecca Elliott?" he smirked. "It was only a matter of time before evidence was produced to bring you in. However, you seem to have saved us the trouble."

Mark foraged in his pocket for the gun. "Take me to her, you arsehole," he demanded, willing his hand to stop shaking.

"I'd be careful if I were you… according to your girl-friend, that thing has a habit of going off of its own accord."

They barged into the canteen. Mark saw Becky hunched over her food tray; her pale gaunt features remained immobile as Mark bellowed her name at the top of his voice.

A cook appeared from the kitchen with a mouthful of food. "What the hell?" he asked.

There was a sudden crack from the pistol and the man staggered forward and landed heavily on a counter top loaded with dirty tableware. The sound of smashing glass added to the normal dining-room noises. None of the inmates looked up from their food.

"No going back now, Mr McKenzie," Scrivener said haughtily. "Give yourself up. Your girlfriend is one of the walking dead and you can gain nothing from this."

"Shut up!" shouted Mark, digging the weapon into Scrivener's ribcage.

He lifted Becky from the chair and cradled her next to him. Her soft skin tormented him like an unquenchable thirst. Her expressionless eyes, like a beautiful porcelain doll, sent a shiver darting down his spine; he felt more alone than he'd ever been in his life.

"You can come with us," he said turning back to Scrivener, "or I can get a canteen knife and cut your bloody hand off to open all the doors!"

They met no resistance on their way back to the car; the prison was like a morgue.

"You must realise that you are a condemned man," were Scrivener's last words as the car door lowered between them. The vehicle sped from the car park, breaking through barriers in its path.

She sat motionless beside him, her gaze focused on the hands folded in her lap. "I love you, Becky," he said. "Please hear this... I came to rescue you... I came in the end," his voice faltered. He sighed at her lack of response as his foot jammed down on the accelerator. She was broken and he couldn't fix her, but only she could ever fix him. "I just want to be with you... nothing else matters," he whispered.

The cliff car park was empty but for one or two cars. Mark grabbed Becky's hand and manoeuvred her into a clumsy embrace. His lips brushed hers momentarily. "I failed you Becky, and I'm so sorry." He looked into her dull, vacant eyes, hoping for some tiny response. "I did this to you, just as much as if I'd put the needle in your head... please forgive me?" Her body remained limp and static, mummified by the coarse prison cloth.

There were sirens in the distance. He tore himself from the vehicle and swept her out of the passenger door, leaving it abandoned like a broken eagle. She walked quietly beside him, all the way to the summit. Although it was daylight, the tunnel was dark and foreboding. As they emerged on the cliff face, the sun rolled out from a cloud suddenly, like a torch from heaven.

Mark turned to her. He could smell her fragrance beneath the harshness of the carbolic soap. "It's time to say goodbye properly, Becks," he said, holding her shoulders square so that her hollow eyes aligned with his. "You have to come with me, so we can be free," he pleaded.

As his foot slipped off the edge he pulled her into his arms and, just for a fleeting moment, her blue eyes illuminated in recognition. As they fell, words left her lips that he couldn't quite hear, but he knew she said: "Mark." It was so good to hear her voice again; for a brief moment he was flying before everything went black.

Mark stirred to the sound of metal instruments clanking next to him. Above him there was a white ceiling resembling a plastic bubble. His body was infested with pain, but he recognised he was high on morphine. A cold liquid was being smeared over his left temple.

"Good morning, Mr McKenzie, so nice of you to join us."

About the author

In the past few years, as her five children became more independent, Jeanne Davies began writing fiction and poetry in her spare time. She's since had several short stories published in competition anthologies, and in 2013 won first prize in the Earlyworks Press Flash Fiction competition, with one of her very first pieces.

Jamie's Father

Edward Fraser

He's always been a fighter, Jamie's father. One wouldn't know it to look at him – he's a rather frail man to tell the truth – but he's a fighter through and through. What's more, he's fighting all the time; even now, standing in the corner of his kitchen, dressed, as usual, in brown corduroys with a grey shirt, a pink tie and a tweed jacket. It's a professor's jacket, with black strips of leather sewn into the arms at the point of the elbow. Spectacles, which look quite as flimsy as he does, are perched on top of his long, grey mane and his watery blue eyes stare freely, without mediation, around the room. Outside the birds are just beginning to wake up, and the gentle winter sun is spreading out her morning's glow. Inside, an old man stands quite still. Watching. Waiting.

It's half past seven by the time Jamie makes it downstairs. His father is standing by the kettle with his palms flat out on the kitchen table. In front of him on the yellowing tablecloth is a cup of tea.

"Morning," he says as Jamie enters the room, "cup of tea?"

"Morning Dad, yes please." Jamie drains the contents in one, deep gulp. He manages to suppress a shudder with practiced ease. He doesn't mind that it's cold – in fact he's grown to quite enjoy it that way. It's the sweetness that kills it. He might have liked it as a child, but that's a long time ago now.

He takes a seat opposite his father. He picks up a paper from the sideboard and flicks it open to the sports section. He's holding it three quarters of the way down each side, like his father taught him, so that the corners bend backwards and do not crease.

His father is still standing. He won't sit down. His hands – those writer's hands – like to be busy, and they wander across the surface of the table, weaving pretty patterns; typing distant words that only he can see. Presently he notices that the dishwasher is beeping.

"Did you put the dishwasher on?" he asks.

"Yes," says Jamie, not looking up from his paper.

"Why?"

"Because the dishes were dirty."

"I don't remember them being dirty."

"Well they were."

Jamie's father accepts this without further question. Whistling cheerfully he sets about unloading the clean dishes into cupboards. He completes the task quickly, even faster than yesterday. Now he has nothing to do. For a while he is content to wander about the kitchen, from sink to cooker and back again, but he soon tires of the activity and returns to his perch by the side of the table.

"Is it Sunday?" he asks, after a while.

Jamie is still trying to read his paper. Always trying to read his paper.

"No it's Monday."

"Yes I know *that*... I was talking about your organ recital? Is it on Sunday?"

This question takes Jamie completely unawares. For a minute or so he doesn't answer, but just stares at the headline on page 7, 'Wazza does it again', thinking carefully. "Yes it is – why do you ask?" he says at last.

"I'm wondering whether Mum will make it back in time, that's all."

This time Jamie does not hesitate. "I'm sure she'll make it back in time. She always does."

His father does not seem convinced. Suddenly he is at

78

the window, squinting out onto the lamp lit street through a gap in the curtains he's made with his hands.

"I think I should go and pick her up. She should be back by now. Yes I should pick her up, that's what I should do... I'll have to take the car, are you all right walking to school?"

At last Jamie looks up from his paper. Dropping it with a sigh, he walks around the table to join his father at the window. He takes his father's hands in his own and moves them away from the curtain, which falls shut again to secure the house once more from the outside world.

"Listen to me," Jamie says. "Mum will be back in time, don't worry. She wants you to wait for her here. Remember what I told you? She doesn't want you to leave the house. You mustn't leave the house."

The old man's brow briefly furrows in thought. Then his face clears and brightens. "You're right Jamie, I remember now... Yes I'll wait here, shall I? Maybe I should clean the place up for her, cheer it up a bit. Come on, what do you think?"

"I think that's a great idea." Seeing that the confusion has passed, Jamie returns to his seat and his paper. No sooner has he turned a page his watch starts beeping. Eight o'clock; time to go already.

"Got to go. I'll be back later. You wait here for Mum," he tells his father, getting to his feet.

"Right, see you tonight."

Jamie picks up his briefcase and gets to his feet. He's nearly reached the front door when his father pipes up – "Wait, you've forgotten your lunch money." Right on cue – funny what the old man remembers. Jamie turns around. His father has his wallet in his hands, and his fingers are plumbing its depths, looking for loose change. Jamie waits patiently, one hand outstretched in front of him, the other clasped around his own wallet thrust deep into his trouser pocket.

The search is taking longer than usual. Too late Jamie realises what he's forgotten to do. He opens his mouth to say something, but there is nothing to be said now. His father is still looking but he won't find anything; nothing was left for him to find. He's getting more and more agitated. Quickly he becomes frustrated by his failure. "It is always here," he says. "Where is it? Where is it?" The wallet drops to the floor through his shaking hands.

For a while both of them stare at the ground in silence. Then Jamie's father bends down to pick it up. Their faces meet, and Jamie sees the shame in the old man's eyes.

"Dad. Dad. *Dad!*" he says. "Don't worry about it. It'll be fine; I've got some money left over from what you gave me last week."

Jamie's father rises. All memory of anger has vanished like smoke in the wind. He smiles at his son. It's a lovely smile. "You're a good lad. I don't know what I'd do without you." He hugs him. Jamie is smiling too now.

"Have a good day," his father says.

"You too, dad."

Roger from accounting is waiting for Jamie when he gets to work. Jamie spots him loitering around outside the main entrance, and he initially manages to evade him by taking the longer route to his office, but the escape is only temporary; the persistent jerk ambushes him by the water cooler one hour later anyway.

"Are you all right mate," he asks, leaning with one hand on the water cooler and the other cupped under his chin. He shuffles forward for maximum effect. "I mean, *is everything okay?*"

Jamie ponders the gravity of this simple question in

silence, wishing that the water ran faster, or that he had never left his office. He doesn't take his eyes off the paper cup he's holding under the tap. In any case he knows without looking that Rodger's expertly groomed features have been carefully arranged in such a way as to convey to anybody watching the maximum amount of polite concern. That's why he talks so loudly when he's with Jamie – he wants the others to know what a great guy he is. He doesn't care – not really – if he did he would ask him about his father specifically. His enquiry is too vague. It is too general. Roger is ticking the boxes; he is reassuring himself and everybody else that he is a good bloke.

Jamie glances up at him. He has caught the eye of Katherine, the pretty, blonde receptionist, who is simpering at him from behind her desk. Roger is clearly rather happy with himself. He runs a hand through his slick, greasy hair and, noticing Jamie watching, flashes him a wink.

"That a boy, it'll be all right."

The musk of the man's aftershave is overbearing. Jamie doesn't know why he does it, but there's something about the look on Roger's face that he can't stand anymore. He empties the cup of water over his chest.

"What the hell man!" Roger's hands are all over his soaking shirt, trying ridiculously to rub it dry. Without offering him an explanation Jamie turns on his heels and hastens to his office at the other end of the hall. The aftermath of the disturbance reaches him even there. He can hear Roger's voice – "That's the last time I try to help him," and Katherine's – "Ignore him, he's a jerk. He thinks he's the only one with problems." He closes the door to his office and removes himself from the noise. He's smiling. That felt nice. If only he'd had the thought to leave a parting shot. Something smart, like, "clean yourself up, mate, you're a disgrace." That would've been good.

It's not until he's been sitting at his desk for several minutes that he begins to contemplate things a little more seriously. He knows his father wouldn't be happy with him. "Ignore them," he'd say. "Just ignore them. Who cares what others think. It's you and me son, that's all that counts. I need you focused and by my side if we're to beat this thing, not worrying about what a stranger has to say."

But wait a minute – screw that! It's easy for him to ignore the jibes – he doesn't have to hear them, and he wouldn't understand them even if he did. It's Jamie who's on the front line, so to speak. It's he who has to deal with all the crap. The old man is happy as Larry in his fairy tales and has no idea most of the time that anything is wrong.

Jamie sits quietly fuming for several minutes, taking out his frustration by repeatedly stapling a piece of paper to his desk and imagining it's Roger's face. Gradually, he comes to his senses. He sighs. His father is right, of course. What he has done just now – that is no way for a man to behave. He's let his father down. He'll make sure he apologises to Roger before he leaves work.

Jamie returns home late that night following a rather embarrassing conversation with a certain co-worker. He walks straight into the living room, expecting his father to be sitting on the sofa in front of Coronation Street, but the sofa is devoid of company and the T.V. screen is blank. He picks up the remote from the sofa's arm and, switching on the T.V., stands watching the adverts.

"Dad?" he calls, still staring at the T.V.

"He's in the kitchen Jamie."

Jamie wheels around and very nearly throws his brief-case across the room. He'd not noticed the two ladies at the back of the room. One of them – the one that had spoken – is Karen, the nurse who cares for his father every other Saturday when he's out of town with work. The other is Miss. Roberts, a nasty old bag from No. 8, just down the street.

Karen's a sweetheart, really. She's about as old as his father – maybe in her early fifties – although she doesn't look it. She has thick, brown hair which she wears scraped back from her head in a ponytail. Jamie's never seen her outside of her blue nurse's uniform, so it's just as well the colour suits her. Unlike Karen, Miss. Roberts is not a sweetheart. Bitter and twisted, she has remorselessly haunted Jamie's family ever since his father's diagnosis. She is a tiny thing, with gnarled, silver haired hands and a long, witch's nose.

Karen has got to her feet and is hovering uncertainly, apparently unsure of whether she should sit or stand. Miss. Roberts, on the other hand, continues to make herself quite at home, installed deep inside what used to be Jamie's mother's chair. She even smells a bit like a witch; slightly stale – a forgotten tennis ball lying at the bottom of a bag.

"What's going on?" Jamie asks Karen apprehensively – she rarely brought good news.

"Your father has had an episode. He was in the middle of the road when Glenda found him. And thank God she did – who knows what would have happened."

Little Miss Roberts was trembling. "I couldn't get a hold of you Jamie. I had to call Karen – I didn't know what else to do. The whole village was watching!" She looked thrilled by the prospect of a scandal.

Jamie excuses himself and leaves the living room. As he nears the kitchen, his father appears in the frame of the door. "I told them I was waiting for my wife, but they wouldn't listen," he says.

Karen and Miss Roberts come to join Jamie, the three of them crowding around the entrance behind which his father has been hiding. From the meaningful exchanges going on behind his back it is clear to Jamie that the ladies want to talk to him alone. It comes as no surprise to him, therefore, that Karen, standing on tiptoes to peer over his shoulder, advises his father to go to bed.

"You should go upstairs, Frank you're quite tired aren't you?"

"Yes, it's time for bed," adds Miss. Roberts quite unnecessarily. She annunciates each word as if she's dealing with a simple child. Her patronizing smile starts in the very corners of her beady eyes and spreads all over her face, which she has bunched up like a cabbage.

Jamie's father looks at him. "What do you think, Darcy?" he asks.

Jamie's face stiffens, but otherwise he pays no attention to the accidental slight. He isn't ready to have another chat with Karen, but, since this is clearly what she wants, he sees no point in delaying the inevitable.

"It's up to you Dad," he says. "If you're tired, go to bed. Are you tired?"

At first Jamie's father looks uncertain. Then he smiles and yawns. "I am rather, now that you mention it... Yes I think I'll go upstairs, night all." And with this, the old man traipses up the stairs to bed.

"Who's Darcy?"

Karen, Miss. Roberts and Jamie are sitting in the living room. Karen is looking at Jamie, and Jamie is looking at the floor. Miss. Robert's eyes are roaming greedily all over the room, taking in every shabby detail – from moth eaten curtains to peeling wallpaper – in preparation for

84

spreading the gossip about the village.

For a while Jamie does not respond. Then he says: "Nobody. A character in one of his books."

"I see. And does he often confuse who you are?"

"He's a writer. He's always been like that, living in other worlds and things."

"But he hasn't always called you Darcy, has he?"

Jamie says nothing. He begins picking absent-mindedly, at the loose fabric on the back of the sofa.

"You shouldn't let him do it," Karen continues. "It's important that you try to keep him in the real world, or else his fantasies will become his reality."

Still Jamie says nothing. He's wondering what about the real world is so worth keeping.

Karen looks serious. "Jamie this is no longer something that you can continue to manage by yourself, at least not if you want to keep working. Your father needs twenty-four hour a day company; he simply cannot be left alone. You were lucky this morning that Glenda was able to stop him from leaving the house, otherwise anything could have happened to him."

"That's right," Miss. Roberts says importantly, a claw gripping the arm of her chair. "It was horrible; I didn't know *what* I was going to do!"

"I'm sorry to have put you through all that," Jamie bursts out, scathingly.

Miss. Roberts doesn't miss a beat. ""That's quite all right Jamie," she replies. "I just wish you'd told us that he was *that* bad."

Jamie stares at Miss. Roberts for a while, imagining cruel and unmentionable things, before he turns back to Karen. "I can manage," he says, "I have always managed. My father will be okay. He's happy here with me."

"But he's getting worse isn't he?" Karen insists.

85

"He has good days, and bad days, like anybody else."

"Jamie, I'm worried about you – you can't continue to live as you have been living. It's not fair for you to carry the burden alone."

Jamie swallows the lump that is rising in his throat. He likes Karen – she's always been kind to him – but he won't let her take his father away. "I'm fine," he says, "don't worry about me."

Jamie can see the corners of Miss. Roberts' delicate mouth curving incredulously. Clearly she doesn't believe him. He's heard them all talking, of course. "I don't know what he thinks he's doing," they say to one another, "trying to look after his father by himself. He'll never manage." As if they have more of an idea how to cope. As if they have any idea at all.

Karen is talking again. She's leaning forwards now, and becoming quite animated. "Jamie I would like to talk to you about the possibility of taking your father into our care on a more permanent basis. You know he likes it at Hardlow. There are people like him there. It could be a home for him."

"Please don't call it a home," Jamie interrupts. "Call it anything, but don't call it a home. A home is where you live; the place you are talking about is a place you go to die."

"Won't you consider it?"

"No – absolutely not. I can care for him quite well enough here. I appreciate what you're trying to do for me, Karen, but I can't turn my back on my father. I told him that I would look after him until the end. We are going to fight it, he and I."

"It's degenerative Jamie, you know that don't you? It will worsen over time, and quickly too, now that he is in such an advanced stage. Our nurses – they know what they're

86

doing. They will look after him."

"Will they though? Or will they not be able to find the time? I know how busy these places are. I do not want my father to be forgotten."

"Hardlow is not like you might think. Plenty of people are happy there."

Jamie doesn't reply, and so Karen, apparently unwilling to give up, tries a different tact.

"Weren't you at Oxford?" she asks.

Jamie glances at her, suspicious. "No, King's College London."

"Psychology?"

"Philosophy."

"Yes that's right. Wouldn't you like to go back?"

"Well sure, but I can't now can I? Not while my father needs me."

Jamie sees the trap before Karen closes it around him. "He wouldn't want you to put off your future for him. If you let us help you then you can go back and finish your course."

"No thank you, I would rather stay at home."

"Listen to me Jamie; whatever the two of you have agreed, you cannot beat this. There is nothing you can do. But we can help you; we can manage your father's decline. But you have to let us. Please let us take him off your hands.

For a long while Jamie is silent. Then he shakes his head. He's my dad," he says simply, "and I promised to stay by his side."

Karen sits back in her chair. Her soft brown eyes are swimming with pity. "All right," she says, palms out-stretched, "you win. But you have my number, don't you? I'd like you to give me a call any time you want. Never forget that you do not have to be alone."

87

"Yes, you are not alone," pipes up Miss Roberts from her armchair, eager to make it her business. Jamie ignores her. He takes Karen's hand and shakes it.

"Thank you," he says. "But I'll be fine."

"Lay the table, Jamie, there's a good boy! Hurry up lad, it's nearly ready!"

The kitchen is a piping mist of activity. Although it's a Thursday evening, the whole house resounds with the sounds and smells of a traditional Sunday roast. Jamie's father is putting the finishing touches to a fine looking chicken, which he's preparing to serve with all the trimmings, no holds barred. Amidst the swearing and the clattering of a man at work the sweet scent of Rosemary fills the air.

For a good hour or so Jamie has managed to keep out of the thick of things, but, in spite of his commendable effort, he's not able to avoid being drafted in for the grand finale. On his father's instructions, he sets about tidying things up. There are utensils all over the place; his father has always been a messy cook. Discarded dishes and baking pans have been thrust into the sink. The cold tap must have been running for quite some time now, for, although it is only ever so slightly on, the water is nearly overflowing. Jamie turns it off. Next he takes the gravy, which is spluttering in a pot on top of the oven, off the boil and pours it into a jug. He can smell the potatoes in the bottom oven, getting that last bit of crisping out of the way. Spread out all over the wooden work surfaces are bowls containing various vegetables; carrots and butternut squash from the garden and cabbage and broccoli. He places these bowls in the middle of the table and, taking cutlery from the draws, lays two sets of knives and forks at either end.

His father turns around from the side by the kettle, where he's tending to his chicken, to survey his son's handy work.

"You're missing one," he says, nodding to an empty chair. "Where's Mum going to sit, on the floor?"

After the slightest pause, Jamie goes back to the draw and lays an extra place.

"It won't be long," his father promises him. "Get the potatoes, will you, they should be done by now."

Sure enough five minutes later dinner is served. Jamie's father has provided from somewhere two long, thin candles, which are flickering in the middle of the table. He is sitting at one end and Jamie is sitting at the other. Jamie is about to begin when his father frowns at him.

"Come on, let's wait for Mum."

Jamie looks at his father carefully. "I'm not sure if she's coming," he says.

"Oh she'll come – just you wait and see my boy."

Jamie opens his mouth, but closes it again without a sound. He doesn't have the heart to argue.

So the father and son wait. Though the candles burn dry and their supper grows cold, still they wait. All the while the old man's hands are restless as ever; all the while his eyes are roving around the room in a fitful search for his wife. Then, just when Jamie feels he can bear it no longer, he realises his father's eyes have stopped moving. He's staring at the floor now and his hands are clasped on his lap, his thumbs pressed so tightly together that Jamie can see the whites of his knuckles. When he speaks it is with such a hollow, beaten voice as quite robs the breath from Jamie's chest.

She's not coming home, is she?" A moment of piercing clarity – fleeting but real – a reminder of life behind heavy eyes. Jamie can feel the tears welling up. He'd told himself he wouldn't cry this time. With a great effort he keeps his voice from choking. And once again he tells his father: "No dad, she's gone."

It's five months later and Jamie is going to see his father. It's Saturday but Jamie isn't working; he doesn't work on Saturdays anymore. He doesn't work very often at all, in fact. His father isn't well, and he doesn't like to leave him on his own.

Above the entrance to a large, cold building, a tired sign hangs loosely, spelling out the message 'Welcome to Hardlow' in peeling letters. It's a harsh reminder for Jamie, lest he forgets his failure.

What he's never been able to understand is how the place can smell so clean. It's so tidy too. Where's the mess, the tell-tale sign of life?

His father is sitting by the only window in his empty, white room when Jamie enters. He does not turn around greet his son. Jamie comes over to put a hand on the back of his father's wheelchair. Softly he kisses his wispy head. Nothing – not even a whisper of recognition. Maybe he's off in one of his fantasies, ever the writer. More likely he's thinking nothing at all.

The old man's features look nothing like him. His face is gaunt and his body is twisting this way and that, as if he's in pain in spite of all the drugs. Skin stretches tight over hollow cheeks; empty eyes stare ceaselessly from sunken sockets – staring, but never seeing. It's all about the mind, really, that's what controls everything. Once the mind goes there's nothing left but empty space. He doesn't even smile anymore. It's such a shame – he had such a lovely smile.

Until a couple of months ago there had been days

when Jamie's father had still been able to surprise him. The elusive high of an occasional memory – such a thrill – for a moment it would taste like home. Then he would fade away once more and the grief would be felt again, stronger this time than all the times before. And Jamie would be off through the corridors wandering, wondering what he might have said, what he might have done to arrest his father's slide.

He's learned now that there's nothing he can do to help his father in his struggle to remain a person. Robbed of his sense of self, the old man is condemned to drift aimlessly through eternity, like a ship without a captain, and Jamie is powerless against the waves. He's a spectator really, that's all, standing on the beach amidst the wreckage carried ashore by the swell of the tide.

He remembers that last lucid moment – he'd been sitting just here, his father lying in his bed beside him, his chest rising and falling uncertainly with each snatching, painful breath. Jamie had had to bent right over to catch his words.

"How much longer son?" He'd asked. "How much longer will it go on for?"

Jamie had not known what to say.

Presently a nurse walks in without knocking. "Time for your medicine," she says. She's a middle-aged woman and her wide face is not unkind, but her smile is empty and business-like. She pounces upon her patient at once, sparing no time for manners. She takes the medicine in one hand and squeezes her other hand around Jamie's father's mouth to force an 'O'. Jamie watches in silence from the chair where he's sitting, a few meters away.

At this point Karen pokes her head into the room.

"Bryony, could you change Mrs. Ryan's bedpans when you get a chance?" she asks.

Bryony nods. She's still trying to force Jamie's father to swallow his medicine. Jamie is pleased to see that he's making her struggle. His tongue is flapping wildly around his mouth in a desperate attempt to repel the invasion.

"Argh!" Bryony sighs with frustration. "Yes of course Karen. I'll just finish up with this one, then I'll jump right to it."

This one. Jamie looks at Karen and Karen looks at the floor. For an instant Jamie can see the shame, but then she is gone; even Karen has other things on her mind. Jamie stands up.

"I'll do that, thanks," he says to Bryony. "Why don't you go and see to Mrs. Ryan?"

Bryony smiles more brightly than before and, thanking him, follows Karen out of the room.

Jamie takes the medicine that the nurse has left behind. As he draws level with his father's face he notices with a gasp that a flicker of substance has returned to the old man's expression. It's very faint – in all likeliness the nurse would not have noticed – but Jamie pays attention to that sort of thing. So suddenly his father is staring at him, begging him frantically through bloodshot eyes. And Jamie realises that if he had a voice he would be screaming, from the depths of his lungs he would be screaming – "Please, let me die."

He pauses. His father has been so brave throughout it all; so brave it's unbelievable. "We'll fight it Jamie. We'll fight it together," – that's what he used to say, the crazy fool. Once upon a time Jamie had believed him. But that was then. Now he looks afraid. Just a boy, running from shadows.

"I'm still fighting Dad," Jamie whispers. "You're not, are you?"

The world is cruel; Jamie knows his father should

have died a long time ago. In this moment he understands what it is he must do. Tucking the medicine into his pocket, he stands up, he puts on his smile, and he walks away. *Not long now, dad,* he thinks. *It'll be over soon.* He will never know how much that means.

About the author

Details of Edward's writing are found on his blog: www.theedexperience.wordpress.com. His stories focus on people in extraordinary circumstances.

He is published in *Philosophy Now* and is the writer and co-host of the popular philosophical podcast 'The Thirst' (www.thethirstpodcast.com).

He has a particular interest in the British empire from 1815-1918, and the First and Second World Wars.

He is keen on travel and on Manchester United Football Club.

The Inventions of Mr Pitikus

Alison Lock

The wind blew all the time; it was a fact. Plants and trees grew horizontal to the ground. In summer the soil was scorched by the sun and the sand storms wrecked the island with spasmodic twister winds that ripped through the earth. In winter everything became elongated, not just the hours of darkness but the sound of the unremitting race of the wind. Icicles stuck out sideways from fence posts and became long shards of glass often to the misfortune of the birds that flew into them and remained there pierced through the heart. A cow had escaped from a shed and within a few hours it was pinned against an iron fence; it's ripped flesh flaunted by the wind.

The people of Windblatter built their houses so that the roofs bowed down to the ground on the windward side. The only daylight filtered in through the narrow slit windows on the lee. Each house had metal-bonded ropes thrown over them and pegged into the ground and fixed there with an aggregate of granite and burnt lime. Fireplaces were boarded over in the winter when the winds were at their strongest because there was little point in lighting a fire when it would be sucked up and away through the chimney. Rooms became burrows as people dug further into the ground where the temperature was constant.

For food, they mainly existed on the mushrooms that grew in their cellars along with a little meat and milk that they exchanged for their wares. Once a month each family would pack up their cart with woven cloth, hammered metal pans, hand-made clay pots or whatever it was that they produced. Each house had a speciality. It took three men or more to drag the cart to the Great Barn where the Trading Post performed all their mercantile transactions. In winter the men could be seen in the streets wrapped in white scarves that went around their bodies, necks and heads. They looked like zombies with their stiff, stooped demeanour. Such precautions were necessary to stop the acid effect of the wind as too much exposure would blind them.

By fermenting their excess mushrooms they found they could produce liquor that was stronger than any of the whiskey that floated ashore from the wrecks. They cursed many a ship for successfully negotiating the rocks in the storms; their rich pickings sailing by just out of reach. The long winter nights were spent supping their mushroom wine after putting a drop or two in the children's bedtime drinks. It helped the little ones to sleep through the dreary hours where the constancy of the whistling wind filled their sleep with nightmares. For the adults, it was easy to overdo the drink and the wine had an uncanny effect of causing hallucinations of the fantastical kind that meant they were reluctant to return to the daytime world of Windblatter. Understandably, they would have preferred to continue with their dream lives of other more fanciful places.

Rollo Pitikus was different. He was not a drinker; he was an inventor who worked day and night on his creations. He kept himself to himself, which was just as well because he was a social inadequate. He could never hold a normal conversation or respond in an appropriate manner. When the kindly souls from the WIC (Windblatter Institute of Cakery) called with their Pat-a-Cakes he waved them away.

"There's no time for that kind of thing here," he'd say. "I've work to do…"

95

Even in the summertime when people were darting between the houses, calling in here and there for The Gossipings he had no interest in the ins and outs of their everyday lives. He was only concerned with the minutiae of the turbines, cogs and rotators that made up his latest invention: the Great Stilling Machine. Seven years of his life had been spent trying to find a way to stop the wind but as with so many of his gadgets and devices it had, so far, resulted in failure. His idea was to make a machine that could suck in the air using its own energy and push it back out again – the same air without the energy. In other words, it would produce still air without the movement of wind. It was not a concept that anyone else could really get their heads around as it seemed unimaginable that air could be anything other than the swift streams that relentlessly billowed around the island.

Now it was springtime and the dark wintering was over. People were beginning to emerge from their homes and hideouts. Mr Pitikus had made twenty five new machines and he was keen to try them out. The idea was to spread them in a line across the island, switch them on simultaneously and wait for the result. He had worked out the precise co-ordinates where each machine should be placed. There were many factors to take into consideration: the geography of the land, soil erosion, the angle of the sun. It was vital there should be no mistakes. He needed the help of the islanders and he knew that now was the right moment to engage them. Emerging from their winter hallucinatory states they could be persuaded to do almost anything even to take part in one of his madcap schemes.

It took four strong people to move each machine; they were that heavy. The furthest they would have to go was five miles and that was over land covered with the meshed clumps of the indigenous Vertiginous Grass with its sword-like blades that could cut a man's foot straight from the ankle. It took many days of hard labour and several returned home with nasty injuries.

Meanwhile, the others who had stayed at home had grown into the spirit of the exercise and had set about making food for an opening ceremony: Chooley pies, Haw Berry Tarts and the famous Windblatter Warble Cake with its iced wind tunnels and candle funnels. They had even made streamers, bunting and chimes to hang about; things that would not normally contemplate. This time they had put their faith in Mr Pitikus's invention but perhaps it was just an over-abundance of hope and optimism.

Eventually, everything was in place and a young member of the community had been invited to switch on the machines. One flick of a central lever would initiate the starting mechanisms of all the other machines. The community gathered around, wrapped up as usual in their cloths and bindings. Behind each mask was a pair of curious eyes focussed on the other side of the island. There was no grand speech, no declaration; there would not be any point, as a single voice would be whipped away before it could be heard.

Mr Pitikus signalled to the child. The switch was flicked and the great turbines began to churn. Everyone watched as the blades rotated faster and faster and they felt the suck of the machines pulling at the wind. Somebody's head gear flew off and momentarily the machines stopped but after a grinding and a whiff of burning they carried on.

Nothing changed for the first fifteen minutes and people were beginning to feel a familiar sense of disappointment.

But then it happened.

Some of them stumbled, tripped and fell onto their backsides as the air was stilled. They looked around at the trees and plants whose tops usually brushed the ground and saw that they were beginning to spring up. People looked at each other and began to speak, amazed that they could hear each other's words without the wind turning their voices into a mere ululation. Slowly, they unloaded their carts of tables, chairs, food and drink and the party began. They waved their cloths around, throwing them up into the sky and watching in astonishment as they drifted back down to their feet. They danced and hugged and ate and drank.

The celebration went on for several days until a youngster, in a state of delusion, ran back into the wind side, surfing and whooping and diving until a current of air carried him into the jaws of the turbines. There was a ripple of shock through the gathering as they all stared at the wall of empty air before them where only minutes ago the boy had scrambled against the force, half in fear, half in exhilaration. The elders gave out stern warnings to all the other young people.

It was not long before one bright spark had a realisation: if they could have half the island back then why not have the whole? A delegation was formed and they went to see Mr Pitikus, who by then was a crowned hero. They asked if they could move the machines over to the edge of the coast so that the whole of the island could enjoy the perfect wind free climate. Pitikus was slightly the worse for wear with an overdose of mushroom wine; in fact, in his mind he was on a tropical island with beautiful girl servants bringing him sweet Jaduboo fruits, the milk of the Coshola and anything else he desired. His great scientific brain had gone soft and slippery and he no longer felt his customary grumpiness. He smiled and gurgled in agreement. Waving a regal hand he said "You carry on, my work is done. Now is the time to rest and play."

So they organised themselves into gangs in order to shift each of the Wind Stillers, as the machines were now known. They agreed to do it simultaneously without switching them off so that their partying comrades would not be disturbed. The idea was to reposition the machines at the far edges of the island.

They were careful to make sure that each appliance was exactly the same number of crow meters apart and at the same altitude as the first positions worked out by Mr Pitikus. They could not risk any runaway wind breakers thwarting the procedure so they checked and re-checked their measurements before heaving the Wind Stillers into their new locations. It was hard labour and took a dozen men to move each machine. They worked together, shouting their instructions along a line that stretched the girth of the island. The result was exactly as they had hoped: the entire island became bathed in a warm windless light.

Unfortunately, just as they were enjoying the fruits of their labours it began to rain. It came in little spots at first and no-one took any notice. But then the rain got heavier and heavier. The people looked up to the sky. They were puzzled. There were no grey clouds so where did the rain come from? And why did it have to rain on the first day of their lives when they could all be together enjoying themselves out of doors?

Rollo Pitikus lay on a bed of Pallumo leaves, his belly stuffed full of good food and every now and then he lifted a bottle to his mouth before falling back into a fabulous dreamy doze. He licked his lips as the rain fell. Even the sky was praising him now with droplets of wine, or was it the tears of the flummoxed wind? It did taste rather salty after all. The rain fell faster and Mr Pitikus slept on but in his sleep his brain began to reform and then a buzz of puzzlement ran through it. He sat up and looked over to his machines, or at least to where his machines were earlier that day or was it the day before? He was not used to feeling the fuzzy after-effects of the mushroom liquor and he began to panic.

"Where are my machines?" he asked in a quavering voice.

"No worries, Mr Pitikus." The young man who spoke looked up at him from an open bowl. His chin was dribbling with seeds of the Cherisha. Mr Pitikus looked at the bowls of empty cocktails surrounding him and groaned.

"Everything's worked out just fine, Mr Pitikus sir," the man grinned and continued lapping the golden liquid.

"Oh no! What have you done? My machines; where are they?"

Rollo Pitikus was on his feet and looking all around him now.

"We moved them to the edges of the island just as you agreed."

But it was all too late. By the time he reached them, they could not be turned off. The salt water had rusted the main lever and all the other switches. By now the island was an inch deep in the sea water that had been sucked into the machines and out the other side. Faster and faster the milled water flooded around them. The energy the water produced was even greater than that of the wind. The streets were filled with floating furniture. Windows were falling in with the pressure of the rising water.

There was only place left for them to go and that was the Great Barn which fortunately had been built on a piece of raised land. Every man, woman and child gathered in

100

the barn. They bolted the doors and climbed up the ladders to the upper level but soon the waters were beginning to seep up between the floor boards.

"We must cut the ropes," Pitikus declared.

They began to argue with each other. For years the ropes had been their lifelines and now they were being asked to sever their cords. They could not see the sense in it.

"If it had not been for your stupid machines we would not be in this mess now," one woman declared. They all turned towards him as he protested.

"It was because you moved them," he shouted.

He jumped onto a pile of boxes behind him to escape their jeers and clawing hands.

"Look, the island is disappearing into the sea. We will all perish if we do not act now."

A sudden rush of water swept through their legs and stopped them on their stride.

"Loosen the ropes," he shouted, "Let's hope the barn is strong enough to float."

The mushroom wine was starting to wear off now and people were looking tired and scared and they could see that there was no other choice. By now the whole barn was creaking and pulling at the guy ropes. It was obvious that if they stayed tethered, the barn would break up and float away in bits and boards and they would all drown. They grabbed the saw blades that hung on the high hooks. With the sharpest blades they cut through the ropes.

The Great Barn began to rise up and tilt from side to side as each rope was severed. Everyone screamed and shouted. Then, all of a sudden they were upright, bobbing along on a calm and breezeless sea. In the background they could hear the gurgling sound as the rotating machines disturbed the deep waters under the ocean.

They floated along for days and nights until they could no longer tell how far they were from the island. The rock they called their home had completely disappeared. Now and again a stray wave tilted the barn and everyone fell against each other as they hit the side. Eventually a brave girl volunteered to be the look-out and she scrambled up onto the roof. She shouted whenever a roller was coming towards them.

"Wave A-Hoy."

The Windblatter folk held tightly on to each other as the shouts become more and more frequent. Finally, one huge wave shoved them up so high that they could no longer see the sea below. Up and up they went. There seemed to be no end to this wave. It was as if they were travelling towards the summer moon until they were held in a cusp of cloud within a pale blue sky. Around them, the air was so still that their breath made no impact. The children blew into each other's faces as hard as they could but not a hair moved. There were no waves, no sudden jolts, just calmness all around them. And under the ocean the inventions of Mr Pitikus churned on and on.

About the author

Alison Lock is a poet and writer of short stories. Her first collection of poetry, *A Slither of Air*, was published in 2011. Her recent publication of short stories, *Above the Parapet* from Indigo Dreams Publishing, contains several stories that deal with how, as humans, we react and respond to climatic and planetary change. She has an MA in Literature Studies and Creative Writing.

www.alisonlock.com

Luggage

Michael Marrett-Crosby

Blind, Moono sensed the murmuring of food. It was enough to stir him. He reached out to his friend and said, "They're eating."

Moono had been lost, dreaming stunted half-stories, all their endings stripped from him by cold. Now he was here, inside the airplane. "We will get there," he said, his words lying like mist across his friend's body. "Together."

His companion did not stir. Moono did not want to either. He switched on a tiny torch and ran the beam around the hold until it picked out his plastic bag. Then he uncurled himself and all the freezing stillness of the metal walls and luggage attacked him. But he knew they had to eat. His friend would wake up for kikwanga, bread made from cassava root, a rubbery lump of home. "Look," he said, pointing with his torch at a bright glimmer in the dark. "See how the water flows for us."

A rill was dribbling down the metal walls. It felt like gift, to find any drink in this steel cell. In the last flurry of escape, Moono had dropped his other bag, the one that had the water. "Remember how we ran?" Moono smiled down at the sleeping head. "We were so lucky."

Lucky. The aircraft jerked and his friend shuddered. Maybe he was waking up at last. Another jolt set loose the bread, Moono crawling after it across the skins of cases. He found the loaf against one wall beside a pool of light. It turned out to be water, gathered in a valley between bags. The torch beam bounced off it. It might have been alive. Moono looked, then quickly bent and lapped, in part to quench his thirst but more to break the curse of what he saw there.

"I've got it." But his friend was still again and blanketed by cold. Moono broke a piece of bread and put it to the sleeping mouth. He was acting as a mother might, for a stubborn child. He aped the act of chewing, said, "It's good. You must eat some. It was made for me by my sister. She…"

Should not have been mentioned here. Her face – it had been her face that had looked up from the water. *Forget*, Moono told himself. *Only look ahead.* His sister belonged to childhood and the river where she'd taught him how to wash and name the world, himself first, "You are Moono. That means Bird in our language. Look at the sky."

He had, like all the others. No one wanted to stay. The plane made another violent turn and Moono was thrown against the bulkhead. Strange – the rivers of cloud he had watched and watched as a boy all flowed so straight, so certainly, towards America or Paris.

But not London. That had come later, with the only school computer. It was donated from afar and mostly broken. London – there had been pictures left on the hard drive. Moono had found them and told no one, hoarded his private dream-gold: streets, tall buildings, people. Even the blacks wore suits and coats. So when he'd reached Kinshasa, nine days walk from the river, he had said "London," to his sister. "That is where I am going. There I will be rich."

His sister had laughed. She was living in a room she shared with many other girls. "Do you want to see its money?" for she had some, five London pounds. "Six thousand Congo Francs," she had translated. Moono touched the note. It was creased and had been often used, worth so much and so many times. Moono had wanted to ask her how she'd earned it. But he had glimpsed the deadness of strange men trapped inside her eyes. He smelt their sickness too, or was it hers.

The bread might still have something of her. Moono stroked it for the memory of hands. But it was cold. Instead he ate and then turned to his friend once more. "Try some, please. It's good."

It wasn't. The aircraft dew was mostly fuel and fear. It tasted of the hours spent crouched behind those airport crates, watching policemen's feet, men paid on commission for every stowaway they found. Moono had watched them dragging two girls away.

And it had been as he stared at them that Moono had felt other eyes. He'd had to rummage through the shadows of the warehouse. Then he had seen him, a boy like him, as uncertain as a candle. For a long time neither moved. Only when the rains came did Moono crawl across to him.

"That was where we found each other," Moono said, a story to rouse his friend. "We found that safe corner. Someone had written there, on the wall, *escape*. We made our camp beneath the word. It gave us hope."

Moono had shared his food. The other boy had brought nothing except a whisper, later in the night, "My name is Gabriel."

Gabriel. He was younger in the face than Moono, had a story that he did not need to tell for it was scrawled across his body, welts and two knife slices, stretched across his back. They made an x, marking Gabriel incorrect, 0 out of 10. Moono guessed that these were wounds of mine-work, Gabriel punished then thrown out. Somehow walked to Kinshasa. He had survived the city, too. "Are you a Christian?" Moono asked that night. The name, it was the name.

His new companion, eyes too big for him, said, "I will be anything they want."

105

That was their friendship made. "So will I."

Gabriel's hand slid out from underneath him. "Come on, Gabriel, wake up," said Moono. Then he borrowed his sister's words to him, "You need your strength." She had said it many times as she nursed him back to health after the road.

Moono had questions for his sister. He had wanted to know how old he was – she thought sixteen. Another of the girls asked if he had made a woman happy. "My sister, by the river," he answered. The girl had laughed. But the same girl had come back later, wearing lips taken from a different face. She had kissed him. It had left a stain.

When he was strong enough to travel, his sister had made him promise. One of her men had paid her in more London pounds. She had peeled off her street smile and then had given him the money, said, "Take this. Don't ever remember what we had before."

"What about the river?" Moono had asked. The river – it was their play and childhood, a time they had been clean, a time, too, when his sister had worn clothes that did not sell herself.

"No, Moono. You have no past. It is all future." Later, while beating the cassava flour, "When you are a rich man, come back for me."

"How will I find you?" Moono had asked.

His sister had not looked up. "I will be standing on the street by your hotel."

They had slid fish-like through the city to the waste of railway. It spread at the end of the airport runway. Here she had left him, the torch her final gift. They had held each other.

"Did you come that way too?" Moono asked Gabriel. "I wish that we had found each other there."

The railway – hard days, worse nights, Moono's

106

dreams latticed with iron bars. He had hunted for a way through, had seen only shreds of people, no one lingering in sight, no one complete. Occasionally, from a pile of trash or the burnt skull of a truck, a hand had stretched and felt for him. He'd let himself be touched. But when they grabbed, he ran. He was lithe and they were dying. Meanwhile police prowled the fence. It was hung with banners of torn clothes.

"I found the tunnel. Did you?" Gabriel did not answer. "You must have done. It might have been made for us. We are both small."

The tunnel was where choices ended. It was slimy with old oil. Snaking beneath the runway, Moono had crawled under shuddering aircraft, the land struggling to hold their weight. He knew then that the mud of Africa was weak.

"You saw our chance, Gabriel. It was you who spotted it."

He might be pleased to wake up to that memory. For hours they had been pinned down by a parked police jeep. Then Gabriel had scampered out across the airport concrete. He had spied the open luggage hold. They'd jumped and then smothered themselves with cases, lying still. A supervisor checked. Then came the darkness as he shut the door on Africa. They had felt the heat of the take-off.

Heat. That had been hours ago.

"We are going to a fine place," Moono said. "This plane is for London." The stack of cases moaned. "Shall I show you?"

He set about building a London there, for his friend. Some of the bags belonged to Africans but a foreign case lay near at hand. Moono used his knife to cut it open and pulled out clothes, fine things: a black jacket, a tie, a pair of shoes. Moono was going to dress himself but then asked, "Gabriel, what do you want to wear?" Something moaned; it might have been his friend. Moono pulled off Gabriel's flip-flops and replaced them with the London shoes, too big but no matter – he wedged them tight with socks. "There," he said, "you are important now. You have better shoes than the police." He was going to shake Gabriel awake and make him wear the jacket. But that felt like unkindness. He laid the jacket over him and let him sleep.

There was more inside the suitcase, papers and coloured files, a book as well. A jewelled woman lay draped across the cover. He tore it off; he would keep it, send it to his sister. "One day I will come back," he promised her. "This will be you."

"You're cold."

He said this to Gabriel. The memory of touching him was reaching Moono's limbs, the grasping chill making him slow to understand. Moono needed to excite them both. "Here, look at this, Gabriel." Moono pulled a picture in a frame out of the case. "Look at how these people smile."

Children, two of them, were staring back at him. Only thin glass lay between them. It seemed like nothing to reach through, to feel their faces and their lives. He was almost there with them in London, everything that he had dreamt, and he was starting to talk to Gabriel about their new friends when…

When his frozen mind learnt what his fingers had long known. Moono stopped. He laid aside the picture. He said to his friend, "You are dead."

Dead. Maybe for hours already. Gabriel had never felt those London shoes. "You were…" except Moono could think of nothing he had been except, briefly, a boy, and

108

now forever a body. He was encased among the cases, wedded to the cold. "Where was your river?" Moono asked. "Who was your sister?" No answer came. Gabriel was luggage. He would be unpacked. No one would ever know his name.

Moono turned back to the suitcase. He had seen something in there. He withdrew a presentation box and card. It read, *For Karen – I knew you would prefer something from Heathrow than Africa so I bought this for you on the way out*. He opened it. Something fell. It was lipstick, lipstick with a bright red nib. Moono used it, wrote spreading letters across his friend, *Gabriel*. There – he was a little more than nothing.

Time slid. The torch battery failed. Darkness took Moono. It was worse even than the searing cold. From above came tiny sounds of humans moving and speaking. Moono sometimes thought to make out words. But more and more he was elsewhere, walking back towards the river. His sister tried to chivvy him away but he explained, "We were wrong. Stay here, together. Let us wash in the water. Teach me the names of things."

At some point, he woke. He found the bread beside him, could not eat. He tried to cling on to the borrowed warmth of having been oblivious. The cold was armed with blades, though. It sliced him. He managed to move against the wall. He licked the condensation. The lipstick rolled against his leg and he wrote his own name on himself, *Moono*. He looked back down at the lump that had briefly been Gabriel. There were few things left for him to do.

He thought to paint life onto Gabriel, healthy cheeks and bright red lips. Instead Moono wrote a word above them on the metal, *Home*. Then he gave back to Gabriel his worn flip-flops and made a mattress out of dirty shirts.

109

He rolled Gabriel on top of it and wrapped his friend inside two suits and several pairs of trousers. Then Moono lay down and closed the shroud around them. Gabriel was supple now; the cold had released him. Moono touched him carefully, a final act of reverence. Thereafter he lost himself.

He remembered his sister. She would look for him outside the rich hotels. He saw long vapour-trails of cloud writing words across the sky, *Escape* and, better, *Home*. Last, he wondered about Gabriel. Moono was so cold. He held him tight. They might even have kissed before the end.

They found the boys but not in London. They made the return trip to Congo before a baggage handler dug them out.

Posthumously gay, they came to matter. They were escaping persecution, some English newspapers proclaimed from far away. While in Kinshasa, voices said, "Good riddance. Their sort are not wanted here." For a time both sides spoke of the shame of them.

Just for a time.

About the author

Michael Marett-Crosby has been writing fiction for five years, having previously published several works of non-fiction. His first novel, *Two Thirds Man*, is now with publishers.

He believes that writing can do many things, but one of them, that he aims for, is captured in a poem written by Adam Zagajewski: *Try to praise the mutilated world. Remember.*

Michael works as lead trustee of an international charity.

License for Life

Bunny Vincent (Nina Miralles)

Part 1

It's hot today. We are cluttered together, blossoms of life, sweaty with ripeness, our skins itching to be peeled. Melanie is the first to stub out her cigarette, Vanessa the next. We all vibrate in anticipation; there is youth and malice and sorrow here. Vanessa lights another, and then, yes, there she is – we watch Kat appear on the other side of the street.

For one moment we all hush, only our eyes move. Kat has pale eyes, we all know it, but today, and in the heat we can't be sure of what's lurking behind the bulging spheres of her sunglasses. Her chin is stuck up in the humid air, the hollow darkness of where her eyes should lie seems to snap at us, jeer at us. Her hands are red, clutching the handles of the pram.

Red is for periods. I don't have them anymore, what's the point? I got unlucky, but in any case I was never much of a decent contender for motherhood, I'd been very sickly as a child. But then my back got bent, curled like a banana in a car accident, my skin yellow from years of neglect and despair. My scars are like the rot on the surface. I had a hysterectomy five years ago, no point in periods, they'd never ever let me have a child license.

Red is for "in the red", the debt that was owed us by...? Well who exactly? Fate? Luck? God? The Child Offices Minister? "In the red" meant waiting and waiting, waiting, waiting, although we knew we'd not get back the time and money and effort we had lost trying. Fiona was waiting. Her hand was shaking because she wasn't

111

smoking; she was waiting to see if she'd get a licence. Her freckles were sunk into her bulk like seeds into a strawberry. Her breasts stiff with anticipation, her nerves erect with the waiting, waiting. Fiona had applied for a child's license seven months ago. She was the last girl on the East Block of the estate who had a chance. She was the right age; between twenty and twenty-five, she'd gotten married to a man the right minimum age gap older (men were thought to be too immature to be fathers at twenty and so had to be at least thirty), he had a stable job, they had no criminal records, have survived the six year initial period of cohabitation, (apparently five wasn't good enough, it was the sixth year that was supposed to be the real indicator of a lasting commitment), she'd gone through higher education and had a home and was healthy and her parents weren't divorced. They'd been investigated vigorously, the Child Act Bureau stopped at nothing. I always thought of them as rapists. Their rape stung, stayed with you forever – the violation of your personal life, leaving you with the trauma of what you'd been through. Fiona and her husband had to face the mental and DNA tests next month, were they stable? Were there any dangerous hereditary illnesses?

Red is for anger. We were angry; I could see the Martian fury in the bloody eyes of Clara. Her teeth were bent like tiny chilli peppers, ready to pinch, her head bowed away from the juicy orange sun. Her throat, I knew, was boiling, steaming like a vat of acids, she was wasted in our group, she would have done better running a dog kennel, running a prison, playing sadistic with soft human minds. "She just fucking loves it doesn't she."

Clara's voice was poison to us, trickled into our crimson emotions, the hush lifted and the mumbling, cussing and pulse of malign whispers resumed.

"Typical of Kat, she must know how we all feel."

"Especially since she knows I've been waiting for seven months already, not knowing."

"Yeah she could give you some advice at least."

"As if! She was always a stuck up cow! How they thought she was a fit mother I'll never…"

I light another cigarette, struggle to digest the smoke through my pain, it's like a plum stone wedged in my stomach, a pin in my spleen. I can't defecate the *longing*, none of us could exhale away the disease of *longing* that had bonded with our skeletons, our cores.

Core is for the essence of things, core is for what you are without the extras. We are women, and the core of Woman is Mother.

Kat's infant's swollen paw made an appearance outside the shade of the pram, its microscopic sheen of nail glowing. It wobbled like a royal waving. Wave – for the wave of sighs we couldn't silence; that were provoked. We wanted that tiny hand with every nanosecond of rippling moan. Green, that's what we were too, red and green.

Green is for envy, which went without saying. I could see Vanessa, prickling up like a kiwi, Melanie shifting her pear-body about… I could see us all, stamped by a foot of global magnitude; crushed blades of grass in an odyssey of stunted growth.

Green is also for the army. Camouflage and all that jazz. Jazz is for what we did on Wednesday nights, we had to fill up our time; two or three jobs, bingo on Saturdays, spinning classes on Tuesdays and volunteering at the local Charity fete on the second Thursday of every month. It was camouflage, camouflage for what we'd rather be doing; packing school lunches, buying our little Sally's ballet slippers, our little Tommy's bicycle helmets, putting

113

plasters in the shopping trolley. I always tell myself, "Try not to let it escape that the army is also for unity." We are united, troops of a barren kind, but united, un-alone. Yesterday, chilli teeth Clara had marched into my kitchenette, *"Recent statistics have shown the average number of families given licence to conceive is decreasing every year. In fact, the ever-increasing regulations put in place by the Child Act Bureau have reduced the annual number of children being born by 54%, in the continued bid to produce more stable and able citizens without the unethical use of genetic engineering, as well as to deal with the overpopulation of our cities."* She read to me over muesli and tough black coffee which had a muscular punch, I remember.

"Bastards," Vanessa grumbled. She lived with me, well why not? Family is family, even if she's only a second cousin. Better she live with me than alone, in the room her husband died in. Just up and died, rolled right out of the double bed, his corpse as clean and smooth as porcelain. Heart failure. Heart failure at forty-six, ridiculous. They were scandalously overworked at the factory. I hadn't bothered marrying, not that anyone had wanted me, what for? To toil for someone who wouldn't be allowed to impregnate me? Spinster. Lifelong.

"I know. I know," Clara snapped. She took some of that muscular coffee, *who brewed it?* I pondered. It's easier, to fill up your mind-mug with banal rubbish, then the lonely thoughts might not eat you. Claustrophobic, life on the Block was, claustrophobic with the reds and greens and heat waves. Green is for our platoon, the one which congregates every 8 a.m. for a cigarette on the East Block of the Estate, to watch Kat walk her baby.

What is the colour of hunger? Only the colour of hunger I do not know. I know what red and green are for,

114

I know that blue is for sadness and brown is for decay. We feel these, tottered in a collage of gaudy emotions, but what about hunger? Which colour paints hunger, because that'll be the one. Because if Melanie, Vanessa, Fiona, Clara and I were anything, we were hungry. There was a draught in our existence; we were dehydrated of our duties as women, inverted with the insanity of inability to breed. Our insides creaked with the lack of foetus, empty, craving the taste of embryo. But our applications lay rejected, our DNA blacklisted, our chances scrapped. Eternally hungry. We stalked the Block with famine.

But yet we were spry, we still had sweat highlighting the need in our faces. Our bodies we carried as yet, without the cripple of age. 8 a.m. Kat and the brand new baby, put it in your agenda. But we had to scatter by 8.30, or we'd be watching Matilda go out for her early shop, and we didn't need that.

Matilda we'd already watched transform. She was a good couple of dozen years older than us all and we'd watched her morph from something supple, fertile, with a smooth hide and gleaming thighs to something quite else. Her body had been biodegraded, recycled, we watched Matilda become old, her teeth rock. I remember when I was a young girl and Matilda used to swim in bountiful-ness along our road, spinning her thick, full belly, her skin fluffy like an apricot. But Matilda's baby bled out between her legs before full term and she was never granted license for another. Red.

Matilda's skin folded into a grisly pattern of dried prunes and then, *now*, she'd become totally inhuman. She seemed to renounce all bone and blood. We'd watched her transform, now she'd hobble past, rancid. She tasted bitter and sour and salty all together. And in the evenings she'd

115

sit on the wall, peering into the flying spotlights of the main road.

Vanessa feared ending up on that wall. She'd never walk past it; always take the long way round. She collected pictures, a universe of youth pasted into a catalogue; newborn, toddler, child, adolescent, male, female, Black, Caucasian, Asian... You want to look at the Mothercare range of spring four years ago? Vanessa's got it. She hangs about outside the window, wishing she could melt into the store, disperse and canoodle in the creases of the jumpsuits, so as to once, in her life, feel the tantalizing silk of a baby's skin.

Melanie knew what it felt like – *a baby's touch*. It's on a Sunday, that we link arms; walking from the 2 o'clock cinema show we always go to. We walk through Violet Hill, the long way home. We like Sundays, all of us, Clara, Vanessa, Melanie, Fiona and I, we get a good old stretch meandering, giggling and smoking ciggie after ciggie along to Violet Hill, then onwards to our damn estate. We do it because the tall trees there pull out their branches, nourishing us with shade, we do it because the air isn't as steamy as in the city centre, with the angry motorcars and angry buses and angry concrete walks. We did it because there, was the Garden of Eden.

Garden of Eden, part of history, part of *religion*. Part of God's plan for us when in heaven; heaven – that means paradise. And here, in our poor world, the Garden of Eden was on Violet Hill, and they called it A Playing Park. This was the "good area" of the city, the area where, as Clara had read on that morning, with the muscular coffee, *"the highest percentage of licenses for the past five years have been granted, due to the high level of income and education amid the well to do families residing in this picturesque district."* We liked

116

Violet Hill very much, but Violet Hill did not like us. The Mama's wore knee-length pleated skirts in pastel silks, they had sweet leather sandals. We wore plastic shoes that brought out the stench of our workers feet; we wore synthetic skirts which clamped themselves to our moist legs with the sweat of pointless labour. The Mama's wore wide brimmed straw hats and tied their hair with ribbons like their cherry blossom daughters; we covered our heads with knotted handkerchiefs and table cloths to screen from the sun. The Mama's had Papa's with them, husband and wife, spouse and spouse-ette. Melanie, Fiona and Clara, the married ones out of us had large, greasy, hairy blokes, with rough chins and dirty scalps who only left the factory at nightfall. The husbands on our estate were made out of leather, just like the Violet Hill Mama's sandals. Appropriate show of social hierarchy.

We scuttle through Violet Hill till we get to the Playing Park. And there was our time slice of paradise; pretty Mama's, clean Papa's and buckets full of candy pop children, boys *and* girls, running about, sitting around, squealing, fighting, crying, laughing, digging, catching, mumbling, eating and and and! And last Sunday, before her disapproving Mama could stop her, one little infant girl child had run straight out of the Playing Park gate and grabbed Melanie's leg to stop herself from falling!

Falling; the act of descending. Away from Heaven, back to reality. Down off Violet Hill we'd have to go, back home.

Sometimes the system accused us of exaggerating, told us to be of use to society in a different way, to keep ourselves busy and look after our neighbourhoods instead. But it's not the same. Sometimes they told us how back in the day some women *chose* not to have babies. But it's

117

one thing to choose. Quite another to be forbidden.
Falling. Failing.
Fruitless.

Part 2

We find it difficult to remain silent during the service.
There's a shuffling, the raw cleaning of throats, a throb of
tapping toes, mumbling, tittle-tattling. I think I can even
hear someone humming. It's because of how difficult this
is, for all of us, the red and green army of the Block, it's
difficult, this hurts too, Matilda's passing away.

It hadn't even been dignified. She perished alone, at
the dining table, facing a lone supper. We hadn't noticed
her absence from the estate for a week at least, by the time
we came round to questioning it, a black smell was issuing
from behind her front door. Charlie Crane we sent along,
to break down the door, whilst we alerted the relevant
authorities.

A rude death; her skull smashed into the surface of the
table, her organs already rotting under the surface of her
cold, lumpy skin. Her eyes dry as a tin, her tongue rigid
and swollen. There was no one to take over her flat when
they'd taken her away, so we went in to polish, steal and
exorcise. But the things we took; the pale sun-screening
hat, a string of faux pearls, a soup recipe book, a tall
canister of prehistoric hairspray, an unopened packet of
forty denier grey tights... they all seemed to be coated
with the stench of decomposing. The lingering fog of
cadaver could not be scrubbed off the pearls, lifted of the
hairspray, dusted off the soup recipes front cover. The
smell strolled into our homes, cursing our lives with a
feeling of the impending grave.

We are not young anymore; we have no other path left

to walk. One by one, the items were seen to appear on the weekly rubbish tip behind East Block. The flat was emptied, the door locked. Matilda had passed away.

"Passed away" is past tense, something already occurred. "Passing away" is more like a verb of motion, "in the act of" passing away – it's a lengthy operation. This funeral is difficult because we were "passing away", we were waiting to become the "passed". Waiting, waiting. "Away" is another concept up for debate, in the "away" of "passing away" one was actually remaining. Instead of absence there was infinite presence. We too, would be interred into our belongings, marking ourselves on the air in our space, the digs we'd existed in, because we had no connection to anything living, there was no heir to take over. The flats would be emptied, the doors locked. A row of peeling doors on an abandoned corridor in an overheated, overcrowded city – a matching row of headstones with block capital inscriptions at "Finsbury Burial", a twenty minute trot north. Yes, we'd all aged.

Age, another word implying a time period. What time periods were there for us girls? No wait – biddies. There was birth, certainly, back in the day when that was allowed; there was girlhood and then the final, agonising stretch of womanhood. We are the new Matildas.

There a cold buffet after we see her driven away in her cheap wooden cave.

"Poppet, would you like another cucumber sandwich? I'll get you some more, what is it, beer? Oh okay, yes of course, would you like another napkin? Yes, another napkin would be good, wouldn't it poppet? Melanie is going to get you another napkin honey, hmm yes poppet, yes sweetie." Dull eyed we watch Melanie fussing over her husband, cooing at him, fretting over him. Her voice alone played out amid our midnight robes of mourning.

119

Mourning. When had we started mourning? We did not start mourning this morning, when we put on our formal black tunic dresses, which double up as church outfits, oh no. We did not start mourning when Matilda disappeared from her haunt on the wall. Oh no, we mourned long before, decades before, mourned for all that we knew would come to pass. The haunt of Matilda, the having-nothing-to-live-for curse. Although curse implies magic, which allows for the prospect of miracles. But miracles were void, they were fiction, miracles were absent.

"Okay, poppet? Anything else Melanie can get for you, pumpkin darling?" Why was she talking to him like that, watching for his every need. Melanie, he is a grown man. She'd started doing this years ago, and it had gotten worse and worse. Probably around the time Fiona decided to stop living. Fiona's application for a child licence all those years ago, an eternity of menial domestic chores and minor miseries ago – was rejected. Her husband had a gene which would give the child high rates of something or other illness, I think, though I may be mistaken, that nobody can remember what. She sat down in a chair that day, with the letter in her fist and never stood up again. Rather about the time Vanessa took to adopting stray cats, hoards of them. I haven't heard Fiona talk in twenty odd years. But it doesn't matter; we wheel her into the courtyard and talk at her glazed, grey eyes.

Grey, the least expressive colour in existence, the anti-colour. Grey – the definition of black and white. I could see the grey in all of us, there was grey in my nails, grey in Clara's hair, grey in Melanie's skin. There was a questionable fluff growing about my chin, about Clara's ears – grey. Aged, we are the decaying fruits in the fruit bowl. The ones that belonged in the garbage.

"Garbage!"

Clara snapped, clacking her teeth together as Vanessa read the paper to us, seated outside in the sore and blistering sun, next Saturday. "Why should it be garbage?" I asked quietly. "They're giving us false hope! The system is rot. Everything's rot," she clacked back at me. But it didn't stop her hobbling upstairs with the rest of us, towing Fiona in her chair with wheels to fill out application forms.

"Have you always wished you could have a child? Was your child licence application rejected through no fault of your own? Do you believe you have something to give to a child? Well it just might be your lucky day! In an attempt to appease public outcry over the severity of birth laws, the Child Act Bureau have invested money into a new project. With female suicide rates rising due to women being unable to fulfil their maternal desires, the Child Act Bureau is now going to give away free robot children to childless women who apply. These paragons of modern technology can move, reproduce twenty-three different emotions, speak and even be taught, thanks to a complex system which allows the robot's brain to adapt to its carer's pattern of behaviour. And on the outside, you couldn't tell they aren't real children at all! Of course, the robots can't grow, but they are a fine alternate option for broody women in this modern world."

World is for the space you live in, what's in your own personal space, territory. We wanted to drain some of the grey out of our lives, to inject some colour back into our world. We began waiting, again. But that was okay, this waiting was not apprehensive, it was not existence in fear, under fear of total eclipse, this was in hope, anticipation. We weren't blooming anymore, but nor were we shrivelling. I watched Vanessa knit, clack, clack, clack, the

121

needles colliding to bring teeny tiny clothes to life.

Life, was starting again!

We are smoking outside the East Block, "Hey, we should have a welcome present for our new baby!" Melanie burbled, her words are healthy and well-feed. We'd already drawn up a rota for who gets the robot-child when, we couldn't even now, conceive to be granted more than one! But who knew?! We clapped our hands together, "Hurrah!"

"Maybe a satin-covered cot?"

"Some brand new slippers?"

"A hard-edge learning book?"

And one day I was walking back from work through Violet Hill, my back bawling from pain, when I saw in a window a *beautiful* kitten. It was plush and so tall it came to my waist, the grey plastic eyes seemed to say it, and "I am it. I am what you wanted." Inside I held the huge toy in my arms; the thing was so sleek, crafted with nimble fingers out of real bunny fur. The long wire whiskers cracked on my cheek, in my palm. I ran all the way home, wrestling away the pain in my dead back.

"I've found the welcome present."

So we scraped, if we scraped, we could do it. Clara's stomach moaned at work, because she reduced herself to one meal a day; I could see her eyes watering, as she watched the other women of the estate do their shopping, but she didn't give in. Vanessa had all her cats re-housed, I heard her at night, moaning in sorrow, she said she missed them, it was like having an eye plucked out in a swamp fight. They cost a lot to keep, for days her eyes were plump and pink, but Vanessa said, "It's for the greater good." I worked extra hours till I thought my back would snap.

And exactly a fortnight later, we'd scraped together the money for the kitten toy. Bringing it home I noticed none of us were smoking, but I'd never heard the street ring out with such peals of laughter, never did expectation seems so bright, I could see, actually genuinely see the grey being annihilated out of us. There is destruction going on here and it is not the wrong kind. I could smell the freshness; I could smell the delight being fetched back into our lives. All of me tingled, on the tip of my tongue I can taste something, it's called "everything is going to be okay." That night I slept like a baby.

The next day, we got a letter. *"My regards to all of you ladies... etc... Unfortunately we will be unable to issue you one of the Child Replacement models as you are beyond the age of a natural mother... etc."*

"We're not even allowed to have a fake baby?" I heard Fiona, who hadn't spoken in twenty years, whisper out of the darkness of the hurricane in my head.

And then it was that Kat walked by with her young daughter. Now the daughter's pregnant, six months. We watched them wave to us, the grey ebbing, flooding, conquering. The return of... wave? We look at each other, our pupils loud and dark. We look at Kat and her flushed daughter, with not a shadow on her face. We are an army. The 8 a.m. platoon, green. And we feel red, we want to see Kat's red. To paint our crush, our torment with her daughter's red. To liquidize.

It is hot today.

About the author

Bunny Vincent lives and loves in London, where she likes to explore the boundaries of literature in her own and others work, buy outrageous shoes and drink pink lemonade. She is currently working on a Dystopian novel about the image of women, and finishing a degree in Russian Language. She can be found on her website: http://bunnyvincent.org.

Arevalo

Arevalo

"And ye shall hear of wars and rumours of wars"
Matthew 24:6

In the darkness of the cabin there was a bucket. Half-full of whisky. In it floated a white rag. In the golden liquid it looked like a dormant fish. A few feet to the right of the bucket, two or three wooden crates perched on top of one another and covered with a thin layer of dust were the man's table. On them, a candle flickered and spat light on the rest of the surface. The cigarettes, the whisky and his knife all looked golden and beautiful against the rest, against the darkness that cloaked the cabin and the mountains and the man.

He lit a cigarette, went outside and into the night. A shovel grating the ground filled the air. Then there was the sound of stones or pebbles against metal, and then silence. Somewhere in the distance a dog howled. Then there was the clank of metal and his footsteps trudging back and into the cabin. The man was carrying a metal bucket, half-full of embers. He was holding it with a long metal hook, and the fire inside it shone all over him. Beads of sweat adorned his forehead in the cold night. The glow of the embers filled the space of the cabin now, and the man and everything around him looked majestic in the sadness of it all.

A few feet away from the door a body, another man, lay on the ground. On his back, his arms were stretched to the sides. Deep in slumber, his chest rose slowly and evenly, and his breath was stale and reeked of whisky.

He grabbed a thick wooden plank and dropped it by

the side of the man. A cloud of dust rose, and the face on the floor looked at him as though he were some ghostly figure. He grabbed the body's left arm and tied it firmly to the plank with a leather belt and an old piece of rope. The beads on his forehead were growing thicker now, and they jumped off the tip of his nose. He didn't wipe them off, but took a slug of the cheap whisky and tried not to think.

Resting on the doorway, covered in the dents of time and labour, there was an axe. He took it. In the space of a single breath there was the sound of flesh being torn open, of bones cracking, a howl that filled the cabin and the valley and the moon that cloaked it all. Then there was silence all over, and the smell of charred flesh trickled out of the door. Somewhere, a dog was howling. In the darkness of the valley, the contour of the cabin glowed in its many shades of amber.

The old man tapped the edge of his arm rest and looked up, up to the few remaining stars that were like pearls or diamonds in the sky and which he could not see. With a deep breath he surveyed the air around him and knew that later on it would rain. He took a short, thick cigarette and lit it. With the first puff he extended his legs and smiled to himself and to the stars. His armchair was layers of cowhide and blankets and sheepskin, and sunken in it he took on the appearance of a shaman or a tribal king. It was still dark, but it wasn't night anymore, and there was a cockerel perched on the stony fence that had been built for the cattle and the sheep before the times of the trucks and the storms, and before the tragedies that would come, too. The bird started chanting, and in between the raspy notes the old man heard the earth rumbling, and later the clapping of hooves on the ground and the panting of the

125

beast up the path that led to the creek. He took a long, deep puff and leant back.

The man had ridden through the last folds of the night, and could now see the water moving down, slowly, and the horses that were drinking from it. One or two of them were chest-high in the creek and he felt a pang of thirst overcome him. He dismounted and tied his horse to an olive tree. It had been drinking from the stream for centuries, it seemed, and it somehow made him think of how nothing made sense in that place. He wasn't new to the country anymore, and he had learned that one never gallops straight up to someone else's house. He turned back and looked out to the dry mountains and the folds of the country that he had been through, all glowing now in the morning light. He couldn't see the log cabin or the timid trail of smoke billowing from the open door or the blood or the axe or the bucket that was half-full of whisky and had a hand in it. He didn't see any of these things and he felt relieved. The figures in the sky, which were clouds or frozen winds or falling meteorites wrapping the stars, made him think of the dust raised by a thousand warhorses in battle. Still drained by the blood and the whisky and the howling and the stench he walked. Someone saw him trudging up the path and into what had once been an orchard, and went inside the cabin.

The old man turned to him as he arrived and dumped his satchel on the ground. When the man, now a rider and also many other things he did not know yet, sat down the old man nodded and smiled, as though he could see him. The old man spoke. "Had a rough time earlier on, didn't ya? Heard the squealing," he said, and spat on the ground. His voice was the sound of grit and rusty metal, and as he spoke it filled the valley.

126

"Yeah, rough stuff. Christ... At least he's not awake yet, the whisky knocked him out."

"Yeah, that and the blood the poor bastard must've lost. Anyway, the damn thing's off now. Only way to get rid of the poison once a hand don't look like a hand anymore... I bet it don't look pretty. But it had to be done. Well, that or the arm, right?" he said, and smiled as if he had said something funny and was expecting a roar of laughter.

"Bloody snake... It might look a bit better later, no?"

"It'll always be an ugly thing for him. But that don't matter. It had to be done and if he don't get it now he'll get it later. He'll have to."

"How about a coffee?" the old man offered. He had raised his voice slightly, and his head was pointing in the direction of the cabin. From it, a young boy emerged. His skin was of the colour of the earth around him, and his eyes made the man think of the wild animals he hadn't seen yet, but which he knew lived in the area. The boy leant to where the old man was sitting and put one of his hands on his shoulders. The hand was small and delicate, and against the old man and the many shades of brown in which he was clad it looked as though he was touching a tree trunk or perhaps a mountain. He spoke to the old man. The old man smiled, and a moment later the boy disappeared. He came back a few minutes later with a pot of steaming coffee. The boy poured the first cup and placed it in the old man's hands, which were extended as though he was begging for money or for the grace of god. Then the boy handed one to the man, and again disappeared into the cabin.

"I sent the boy to town last night." the old man said.

"Yeah?" He tried to look surprised, and waited to hear the end of the sentence.

127

"Yeah, he went and got you a few papers. They're from last week, they're old. Old like everything else in this country," he said and paused. He took a sip of his coffee and then continued. "You two were right. Things have changed now." He spat on the ground. "Things have changed for everyone, but I think even more so for you two." The old man put his hand behind him and in between the layers of ashen and earthen hide, he produced and gave him a bunch of rolled up newspapers. There were three or four of them, all rolled up and tied together with a piece of rope. "Here, take them. They're no good for me."

The man felt himself shaking. So did his voice when he spoke now. "Thanks."

"That's alright, son. Now you'd better go and see what's going on in that cabin of yours, methinks," he said, and rolled himself a cigarette.

The one-handed man lay on the dirt floor. It was crawling with small animals armoured in shades of black and blue, and it was also the womb of the cabin. Its smell of alcohol and blood and ash would follow the man wherever it went now. His mind was still not back in the valley but lost in his own self, and in his dreams of gold and red he had visions. Before him danced images of darkness, of hooves punishing the ground and of turbulent seas. The waters of time and force had always dragged him, he now knew, and he didn't wrestle the currents. Deep in the sea, which was black and warm, his body was grabbed by a multitude of palms, of thumbs, of fingers. Deep in the sea, which was black and warm and thick, he didn't dare look down into the belly of the waters. Deep in the sea, which was black and warm and thick and was stifling him, a multitude of hands dragged him down. He then felt a single pair of

128

hands drag him out of the waters and into the valley and the cabin. He woke up. He now knew what he had lost and also that he would never get it back, and his throat opened to let out a wail of sorrow. His head still clouded, he untied himself from the thick wooden plank. It had turned black where his blood had penetrated, and the dent of the axe and its many charred sections made him think of the pillars of a church that had been raided by the hordes. The smell of whisky and burnt wood and charred flesh filled the room, and he dragged himself out of the cabin and into the light. His throat was hide and sand. A few feet to the left, next to an olive tree, there was a bucket full of water. He fell on his knees and dunked his head in it and drank. Drenched in the water and his tears he looked like the survivor of his own shipwreck in the morning light. He yearned for his tobacco, and wondered if he would be able to roll. He lifted his left arm and looked at it. Wrapped in its golden rag and with its stains of blood the forearm looked incomplete and pathetic. It was, it seemed to him, the payment that had once been demanded of him. He had realised once it was too late. The sound of a horse galloping up the hill filled the air in the valley, and he wiped the tears off his cheeks.

"I'm gonna have to learn to roll now..." said the man with the stump, as his friend came to where he lay.

"You know I'm sorry, don't you?"

"Yeah, I do."

"It just feels..."

"I know."

"But you..." He tried to say something, and soon realised that they, or maybe just he, had run out of words, and no sounds or character permutations would help now. "Look at that..." he said to the one-handed man. The sky was crimson rivulets that spiralled down, and in all its

129

horrifying redness it looked like the gates to lands of torment. He went inside the cabin to get a lump of tobacco.

As his friend went inside, the one-handed man thought of hunting again, of the digging and the riding. He thought of the cows and of breaking horses. He thought of the shooting and the building and as he was doing this, the weight of the years past and of those to come sat on his chest. He heard his friend approaching.

"Let's go," said the one-handed man.

"Mmm?"

"Let's go. Let's go to the city. Everything would be a hell of a lot easier there. No digging, no building, no butchering..."

"No riding..."

"Yeah, no riding. But we wouldn't need to, would we?"

"Yeah, I guess so..." he said, and he sunk his hands in his pocket. There was a silence. "We can't, mate," he said, finally. "We can't go back to the city and we can't go back home. And I'm not sure that we can stay here, either."

"What do you mean?" asked the one-handed man, although they both knew what he meant.

"I mean we gotta stay here. It doesn't matter whether we stay in this valley or go somewhere else, but we sure can't leave the country. They've closed the borders."

"You saw the old man?"

"Spoke to him. Didn't look too good and wasn't his talkative self either. But he'd heard some rumours, and he sent that little boy of his to the town to get the papers."

They had known what this meant all the way through, but it was only now that they really understood. The weight on the one-handed man's chest was heavier now, and it was grabbing him by his throat. The other man fetched the bundle of newspapers from his satchel. There was *La Nacion* and *The Herald*. He threw them on the ground, by the one-handed man. They looked at them, and read the same headlines in two languages. The words slowly crawled out of the pages and up their dirty clothes and into their chests. Somewhere in the distance a dog was howling.

About the author

Anglo-Argentine writer Arevalo's work has been published in Latin America, the US and Great Britain. He was a Bridport Prize short story finalist in 2011 and a Poetry Rivals finalist in 2012. In 2011 he created the online literary magazine *Mate*. He now lives and works in northern Italy, where he is working on his first novel.

One Step at a Time

Deborah Rickard

One... step... at... a... time.

That's how Vera did it. Always. And she always got where she wanted. In the end. Today she shifted, one step at a time, around the sun-baked path worn bare of grass by joggers. Perseverance, she called it. Stubbornness, *they* called it; not the joggers but *them*. Which might suggest, quite rightly, that she wasn't going to give in, to *them*.

Oh, she shouldn't be nasty, she told herself. After all, she needed them and "rules was rules" as young Tamara would say. It was hard though; hard to accept you could no longer do what you used to. And even if you could, you couldn't do it when you wanted. It was tough pushing through life instead of skimming along like that young thing flitting past in lycra, diverted from the track by Vera and her life support system; her three-wheeled zimmer-frame. Vera loved to watch the joggers with their lubricated joints sleeking swiftly along. Except... it brought on the yearning...

Unusual name that; Tamara, Vera mused, diverting her thoughts and getting back on track. She'd never heard of it before she came to *The Beeches*. It sounded like tomorrow.

Perhaps tomorrow it wouldn't be so hot and she'd manage her walk a little easier. Perhaps tomorrow she could wear cotton instead of the polyester *The Beeches* preferred because it was easy to care for and never looked creased or old. Fat chance. Tomorrow wasn't really up to much.

Vera sighed as she arrived at the last bench before the

132

final stretch back to the gothic edifice she had to call home these days. She unwrapped her hand from the handle of her zimmer-frame and slowly reached for the arm of the bench; its wrought-iron warmed by the sun. She'd have walked a whole half mile by now, she calculated. Fred would be proud of her.

"Ooohh." She sighed as she eased her crooked back into the seat. She couldn't help it. It just escaped. And out loud too. *Damn!* Still, she was on her own, there was no-one around to hear.

Arthritis. That was the trouble, not old age. She was as young in her mind as she ever was. Well, almost. And anyway, she'd found a way round that little problem. She hadn't told anyone, she'd simply shuffled along to the nice young man in the computer shop on the High Street and bought one of those nat-savvy things, or hi-hats; something anyway, that sounded as if it belonged in a drum kit. He'd even set it up for her so that when she was out walking and got... *confused,* all she had to do was press a button and the lovely lady in the nat-savvy thing told her how to get back to *The Beeches.*

Vera pushed her back against the wooden slats of the bench, breathed in the scent of scorched, dying grass and closed her eyes. The sun shone warm on her wrinkled skin, and bright too, even behind closed lids.

"One final push, Vera love, and we'll be on the summit!" Fred's voice came from a distant remembered land yet sounded strangely close. They were hiking on the Black Mountains; going for the top. No birds sang and no breeze played in the trees. There were no trees, only grass and gorse but from somewhere out of sight a sheep coughed, as if to prove you were never really alone. Vera had laughed with Fred and they'd leapt forward in a race to the top.

133

Of course, they'd both made it. They were never *not* going to make it.

Vera pushed the door open slowly, so's it wouldn't make its give-away creak. If Fred had been here, she thought, he'd have oiled the wheels on her zimmer-frame, and she cursed under her breath as she inched and squeaked across the polished oak floor.

"That you, Vera?"

Damn! Vera thought. "Hello, Tamara," she said. "Just going upstairs, dear, to freshen up before tea." She'd prefer dinner really, not the 'high tea' they had at *The Beeches* but there the matter was. She could smell eggs today.

"And where have you been, Vera? Out to the park again? You know you're supposed to have someone with you when you go out. You should have said!"

And if she had said, there'd be no-one free to go with her. Anyway, she liked to be on her own. On her own she could forget. And remember.

"I'm fine, Tamara, dear. Don't fuss. I'll be down in a little while."

Tamara went back to the day room, back to the in-mates who'd given in and sat doing nothing all day, oblivious to the television in the corner.

Vera pressed a stiff, gnarled finger on the button to call the stair-lift to take her to her other zimmer-frame on the floor above, but the chair didn't budge. It sat at the top of the stairs looking down as if to say "If you want me, you'll have to climb up to reach me." She should ask Tamara to come and help, of course, but...

Vera could see him, sitting in the chair-lift at the top of the stairs. "Come on, Vera, love," he said. "I'm waiting for you!" Fred's smile looked the same as it had on the day they married.

"I'm coming, Fred," she muttered, "I'm coming."

"You can do it! You know you can. One final push and we'll be on the summit."

Vera lifted her foot and hid her pain. One... step... at... a... time, she said to herself.

Vera didn't make it to the top. At least, not to the top of the stairs. Tamara found her a short while later, sprawled next to the stair-lift with one hand reaching out as if clutching at... Tamara knew not what. And there was a smile, such as she'd never seen before, kissing Vera's lips.

About the author

Deborah Rickard trained as a journalist in the 1970s. After raising her children she took up writing again while studying for a degree in Literature, and has since had short stories published in women's magazines and anthologies. She has also had a short monologue performed by the Bristol Show of Strength Theatre Company, and was shortlisted for the Fish Flash Fiction Award 2012. Deborah is currently working on a novel and driving her partner mad.

Family Secrets

Aline P'nina Tayar

It took years for me to blot out the image of Joey McClatchy as he looked the last time I saw him.

It was a couple of days before he died of leukaemia. Throughout the previous week, day-time temperatures shot up to over one hundred. For seven consecutive nights, the thermometer did not drop below seventy degrees. Just as I remembered them doing when we were growing up, at sunset, neighbours came out onto their front verandas to wait for a relieving breeze. But, that week, no Southerly Buster came rattling the Venetian blinds and cooling our houses. Everyone disappeared indoors again, still gasping for air. In bed, the sheets felt as if they were burning my skin.

Yet, Joey's mother had wrapped him up tightly in blankets that went all the way up to his chin, like a shroud. Apart from his big head, there seemed to be nothing left of him. He had always had thick lashes. Now, the weight of them appeared too much for him; he had no strength to open his eyes wide. Nonetheless, he did manage a twitch of a smile when I expressed surprise that he still had on his wall that old Chinese Cultural Revolution poster my father had given him over thirty years before. There was Mao Zedong's bust floating above a group of People's Liberation Army soldiers. The uniformed men's ecstatic faces were all turned heavenwards at their Great Leader. Below them, the caption read "The People's Liberation Army of China is a great school for Mao Zedong Thought."

Since leaving Australia in my mid-twenties, I have been back only three times, one visit for every decade.

136

But, even now, when I get together with a bunch of women friends, the chatter turns to first loves and youthful naiveté and, at such times, I speak of Joey with fondness. He was the first boy I ever had a crush on. Lanky and gauche, he never did seem to get the measure of his arms, even by his late teens when he used to coach me at home in Maths. A sudden spurt of growth at age fifteen had transformed him from the kid with sticking-out, translucent ears who sat cross-legged in the front row in class photos to the boy in the middle of the back row. Even without taking into account the way his dark-red hair spiked up, Joey had grown as tall as a hollyhock. In the final-year photo, you can see the beginning of the stoop he was to develop as a result of constantly lowering his head to the level of his listener.

"Oh, for god's sake, stop it. Stop gawking," my sister, Rosa, would snap at Joey. As if she were truly unaware that a thick clump had broken loose from the hair bunched up on top of her head with a butterfly clip. Of course she knew how beguiling it looked when, with a distracted air, she blew the hair off her face. Rosa was born with a double crown and, as a small child, I had taken that literally because of her haughtiness. What I also understood was that, though our father constantly preached that knowledge was power, beauty was much more potent. Still, I used to say to myself, one day Joey would finally pick up my laser thought-beams willing him to fall in love with me and forget all about my sister.

Joey had been coming to our place for over a year when our father invited him to come with us to the Australian Communist Party Headquarters. These were located alongside the soot-blackened colonnades of Central Station in a poor, run-down part of Sydney.

Rosa had already begun to grumble that someone might see us there even though bumping into anyone from our suburb, on the other side of the Harbour Bridge, was unlikely.

On Saturdays, our family would get together with other Party families to prepare the leaflets which we stuffed into people's letterboxes or handed out on Sundays at the Domain. I don't remember the names of the other children, but I do recall that, when we were very young, none of them worked as hard as we did; my sister, brother and I. After Joey joined us, he was assigned to the same things as us, which included writing out the slogans for the placards. UNTIL VICTORY. NEVER BEEN HAD SO GOOD. NO WAR BUT CLASS WAR.

Our mother drew the caricatures for the leaflets: Robert Menzies, the Prime Minister, aka Old Ming, with his white hair and jet-black eyebrows, as thick and droopy as a spaniel's; LBJ, the American President, with his ten-gallon hat and stirrups, trampling on Vietnam war protesters lying on the ground; the Queen of England with a jutting jaw and a crown tumbling off her tight-curled wig. All week long, our father would sit up late writing the texts which Mrs Phillips, the secretary, would type up on stencils. She was the one who decided Joey should man the mimeograph machine because he was always knocking over paint pots and making a mess. But his hands still ended up stained though now it was in fuchsia from the Olbiterine with which Mrs Phillips got him to daub out typos.

"Joey gives me the heeby-jeebies," Rosa said. "He's too bloody intense. What if he blabbers everything he knows about us to kids at school."

The Domain is a vast green that slopes from the Mitchell Library down the State Art Gallery. It is Sydney's version of London's Speakers' Corner, only that in Sydney you are close to the sea and you sometimes get a whiff of iodine in the air, not traffic fumes. I remember that, in winter, the green was as cold as the Siberian tundra. In summer, the sun stabbed our eyes and made our heads throb. From November to April, Joey always had a scab on his nose from sunburn. In the cold weather, he scratched his chilblains until they bled. Most people waved a hand dismissively at the leaflets, mumbling under their breaths. Sometimes, they pushed us aside roughly or grabbed our wrists and squeezed our arms so hard that we ended up with bruises. As young children we did not see ourselves as taking part in a hopeless campaign. We had, after all, been going to the Domain on Sundays since we were babies in prams.

As we got older, however, we became less immune to what other people blurted out: the Communists and the Trade-Unions were going to take over the country and turn us into slaves. Just look at Cuba. Eventually, Danny and Rosa dug their heels in and refused to risk being seen with our parents anywhere in public.

But Joey remained an enthusiast and, since I wanted him to think of me as more than a kid brought to the brink of tears by Double Maths on Wednesday mornings, I still went to Party headquarters on Saturdays. On Sundays, standing by his side, I continued handing out leaflets. God knows what Joey's family thought he was up to when he was with us, but those were the days when parents still shooed their children out of the house first thing in the morning, admonishing them not to come home until tea-time. When people heckled my father on his soap box, Joey cheered, and I could not help thinking then that my father was brilliant. First, he polished off the Fascists, the anti-Trade Unionists and anti-Immigrants, the Imperialists and the God Squadders who decreed the end of the world was nigh. Then he went on to save the world.

"Does Joey really have to spend so much time with us?" Rosa complained. In the bedroom she and I shared, the desk stood under the window. Even when tweezering the hairs on her legs, my sister would keep an eye out for Joey. If she spotted him at the top of the road, that gave her a couple of minutes to make a getaway through the back door. Sometimes, however, she was not quick enough.

"Ah, Rosa, the Ravishing!" Danny crept up from behind and flicked a beach towel at our sister's legs. "There's a Maths Genius at the door asking to see you." In a fury, Rosa had no trouble overpowering our brother. As she pulled clumps of his hair, Danny yowled. "Shit, Rosy, where's your sense of humour?" His legs flailed about as she sat on his stomach and bounced up and down. What finally shut him up was a Chinese burn.

As a cook, our mother drew on the varied traditions of her family who were scattered throughout the world. You only had to say the name of a country and she would pop up with a name of a first, second or third cousin who lived there, including a cousin in Japan. Danny might grumble that he preferred steak and chips and that he hated the colour green on a plate, but Joey gobbled up everything at our house, which is why our mother often asked him to stay on and eat with us.

"She just feels sorry for him," Rosa said.

But for our mother, pity was a passive emotion and thus abhorrent. "You shed a few tears for the poor and starving people of India and Africa," she said, "but then what? It doesn't mean you're going to get off your ass and do something to help them."

No sooner were we all settled round the table, she

140

would spill something onto the cloth. She did that with all our guests to spare them embarrassment should they knock over a glass or drop a dollop of spinach before it reached their plate. Inevitably, Joey would leave a stain on the linen which, like our solid silver cutlery, was a relic from our mother's childhood in Alexandria. Not that when the Europeans began leaving Egypt in droves did she take away more than one valise. It was one of her uncles, childless and living in Adelaide, who left her all these things in his last Will and Testament.

When my sister huffed and narrowed her big eyes into slits, it only made Joey clumsier. What could I say to make him feel less butter-fingered when all that got me was a kick from Rosa under the table? She was even angrier when, stuck in bed with measles during term-time and left alone to find my own entertainment – we were all expected to be able to amuse ourselves – I knitted Joey a sweater. It was from a Patons and Baldwins *Fair Isle For Two* pattern book and I used wool unravelled from one of my father's old jumpers. On the cover of the knitting book, a male model, who looked like *Dr Kildare*, stood next to a girl in a matching sweater. She was a dead ringer for Lesley Caron who I so wanted to look like. But, I am my father's daughter, big-boned and with a long nose that has a square tip. Rosa, on the other hand, is like our mother, skinny and with fine features.

When I asked our mother how to pick up dropped stitches she said she hadn't the foggiest. "Aren't you the domesticated little creature?" she said, giving me a peck on top of my head. I ended up sewing the holes, making the unevenly knitted sweater even lumpier. Still, Joey said he loved it though I knew he was only pretending not to notice that one sleeve was longer than the other. His gratitude would, anyway, never have been enough to take away the ache of the longing I felt for him.

I'm ashamed to say that whenever hope flagged of Joey ever paying real attention to me, I was occasionally spiteful. I should have, for instance, defended him the time Rosa said to his face that he sounded gormless when he laughed. It was true that the booming ho-hos would well up from deep in his chest and his whole body would shake, but when he looked beseechingly at me to come to his rescue, I shrugged my shoulders and turned away.

"No one in this family seems interested in the Cultural Revolution," our father said when he offered Joey the Mao Zedong poster that Danny had rejected. "My children are turning into philistines."

All their lives, our parents have remained purists. It was hard – and is now virtually impossible – to live according to the ideology of people who had once almost gone to jail for their beliefs. I have heard that story so many times, it is as if I lived those events myself. When Old Ming had called a referendum to ban the Australian Communist Party, Rosa was five years old and Danny four. All Communist assets would be confiscated, and anyone who carried on working for the Party after Parliament had voted a ban would be thrown into prison and, afterwards, never get their old job back. When I was four or five I had a vision of the Angel of Death passing by our house and painting a White Cross on our front door.

Things were so bad that our father, who had not spoken to his mother for more than twenty years, began making preparations to send Rosa and Danny to live with her in the Blue Mountains. It was a tough decision because Granny Sobel was one of those Terrible Trotskyists and, as we children had had instilled in us, Trotsky had betrayed the Revolution. Proof of how much at their wits' end our parents were was that they asked Mrs McClatchy if she would take my sister and brother on the train to Hazelbrook, where our grandmother lived. In the middle of the night, my mother and father went out with spades and dug a deep hole in the back garden at the foot of the gum tree which still stands to this day. There, they buried Engels, Marx and Lukacs.

But, when Old Ming was defeated in his referendum, all the books and pamphlets were dug up again and it was from them that our father eventually came to instruct Joey in Dialectical Materialism. By then, Joey had long since stopped having that trapped-anteater look whenever our father collared him. I remember us all being rounded up once into the living room. It was the middle of the summer holidays and a wind from the desert howled round our house while indoors all that the ceiling fans did was churn hot air.

"Every economic order grows to a state of maximum efficiency." Our father sat on the cool floor tiles while we children formed a semi-circle round him. "As it does this, it gradually develops internal contradictions and weaknesses. These contribute to its decay." For as long as I can remember Rosa has had this capacity to swill a yawn around in her closed mouth and then swallow it without anyone but me noticing. She was certainly able to do that by then.

I've never forgotten the last School Open Day we ever went to as a complete family. Rosa had to be dragged to it after our mother had refused to appear wearing either make-up or a bra. As soon as we entered the assembly hall, our mother made a beeline for Miss Bonner. "I don't agree with your approach to the teaching of History," she said, making all the other parents turn round and stare.

143

"It's too linear." Mrs McClatchy was standing right next to Miss Bonner and I knew she wasn't smirking about linear history but about the way our mother's nipples stuck out under her blouse.

It really was not Joey's fault that people eventually found out our other family secret: our father liked to stand on his head once a day with no clothes on. After he had done his Canadian Air Force star-jumps, also in the nude, he would do a shoulder stand to revitalise his brain cells.

"Oh don't mind me," Mrs McClatchy squished her nose against the wire screen door one evening. "I saw much worse in my nursing days." She must have been the one who spread the story, not Joey, but Rosa blamed him and gave him no chance to defend himself.

"Anyway," Rosa said, "if his mum hadn't been out looking for him, she would never have seen Dad without a stitch on." Now that this even more embarrassing family secret had been leaked, who was to say more would not follow?

We all found it hard to live with Rosa's sullenness so that when Joey won a scholarship to study at Lancaster University in the UK, we were not just happy for him, we were relieved to see him go. Even Rosa came down to Circular Quay to wave Joey off on the *Oronsay*. After that, he and I lost touch and, by the time he returned to live in Australia, I was living in Italy.

But, in the last five years of Joey's life, he and our father became close friends. I would catch glimpses of that in my mother's letters. "Despite the age difference," she wrote, "they are very comfortable with each other. Sometimes, they sit in silence which is only broken by sighs and grunts of contentment, like those that punctuate gorilla grooming sessions. Danny and your father never had this kind of closeness. I dare say your brother wanted

144

to be the alpha male whereas Joey defers to your father and this has a calming influence."

"Why don't you go round and see Joey?" my father suggested on my last visit home. "By yourself. He's bedridden now. There's not much time left."

Joey remembered the old mimeograph machine at Communist Party Headquarters. In a weak, raspy voice he also reminded me of how, after a few hundred leaflets, the stencil material covering the interiors of closed letters such as a, b, d, e, o and p would fall away so that the spaces inside the letters ended up filled with ink. I recalled then how the stencil would gradually stretch, starting near the top where the mechanical forces were greatest, causing a characteristic mid-line sag in the text, which would go on deteriorating until the whole stencil was a complete mess. There was only so much repair with Obliterine Joey could do. Eventually, Mrs Phillips would have to re-type the whole lot. From mid-line sag we got on to the sweater I had knitted Joey. We laughed at how it had sagged half way down his long, skinny thighs. Despite his feeble state, Joey managed to mimic Rosa swilling a yawn then gulping it down without opening her mouth.

"That skill has served her in good stead now her husband is an Ambassador," I said, overwhelmed once more by a yearning for real closeness with Joey. "When her sleeping pills don't work, she lulls herself to sleep by listening to the *Financial News Tonight* on the radio. Dad would disown her if he knew." I liked the warm sense of conspiracy that sharing my sister's secret with Joey gave me, but I could see that laughing caused him excruciating pain in his chest.

After he died, I came across the old *Fair Isle for Two* knitting book in my parents' garage. I see now what I did

145

not see before. The focus of the *Dr.Kildare* look-alike's gaze is fixed on a distant horizon, far, far beyond the shoulder of Leslie Caron's plain little sister.

About the author

Born in Malta and raised in Israel and Australia, Aline P'nina Tayar is the author of a memoir, *How Shall We Sing?: A Mediterranean Journey Through A Jewish Family* (Picador), and a novel, *Island of Dreams* (Ondina Press). Her home is in Bath, but her work is as a conference interpreter which takes her frequently abroad. She is currently working on an anthology of short stories.

Ten Things I Discovered This Weekend

Graham Taylor

At this precise moment in time on Friday 20th March 1981, I am eight years old and have already decided that I hate school. There's far too much writing and general learning going on for my liking. Luckily for us we get weekends off "t' charge us batteries," as my grandad would say.

It's the weekend I'm thinking of as I gaze out of the biggest window in the classroom towards the freedom of the large playing field. Then I turn towards the big white clock above the door and, holding my wooden ruler like a magician's wand, I whisper the word 'abracadabra' in an attempt to speed the hands up so that my weekend adventures can begin.

My attempt fails so I give it up as a bad job and divide my thoughts again between a) how well Boro might do down at Southampton, b) which cartoon they might be showing at the Saturday Morning Picture Club and c) making a list of all the places I'm going to look for my Meccano, which seems to have disappeared from my bedroom all by itself. I'm supposed to be doing my *War Of The Roses* history work, but who's bothered about a load of dead people arguing about a bunch of flowers millions of years ago anyway?

Then Mrs Orr catches me right off guard, scattering my weekend plans and general wonderings all over the place with just two little words that have, in my opinion, no business being together in the same sentence.

"Did she say home-work?" I ask in a whisper, leaning in as close as I dare to the person sat next to me, 'cos she's a girl after all and girls smell. The trance-like, Sarah-Jane,

147

just ignores me and continues to play with her hair.

"For those of you who weren't listening, Darryl, your homework this weekend..." The rest of her sentence drowns out in the loud sea of moans that most of us make in response. Even Sarah-Jane eventually joins in when I tap her on the arm gently with my ruler.

Why didn't I go to the bogs when I had the chance? I could've stayed there 'til home time. Then when Monday morning came round I'd have had a good enough reason for not doing it. Not like Peter the-bogy-eater behind me, who reckons he keeps leaving his homework on the bus, when everyone knows he's lying. He lives right near me and it only takes us two minutes to walk to school, one if we run.

Mrs Orr tries desperately to regain our attention, "It might even be fun," she suggests. The nerve of it, of course it doesn't work, she's lost us completely now. Then she digs a little deeper and her voice gets that tiny bit louder, "Investigating things like private detectives, how exciting."

The room goes quiet, except for the collective sound of thirty or so little brains ticking over. Those two magic little words 'investigating' and 'detectives' does the trick, she's one very clever teacher our Mrs Orr.

"Like Sherlock Holmes," shouts Peter, really loud in my ear.

"Like Nancy Drew," beams Sarah-Jane, now sat up straight with her hair somehow tied up all neat in a ponytail.

"Like Magnum PI," I whisper excitedly to myself, rubbing my ear in a bid to stop the ringing. I think Mrs Orr's on to a winner here and just might be right this time.

From then on until the end of the day Mrs Orr bombards us with stuff about how our memory works and that, hoping that some of it might just sink in. Miss goody-two-shoes, Sarah-Jane, has to go and spoil things by putting her blooming hand up when Mrs Orr asks if anyone has any ideas that might help us remember things. "Making lists," she answers, sitting up straight, all prim and proper like.

"What a good idea," says Mrs Orr. So thanks to Sarah-Jane, not only do we have to remember the new things we discover this weekend, we also have to write at least ten of them down too, blooming marvellous!

As always, my weekend starts at home time. With it being Friday though, I'm usually one of the last to leave, 'cos Mrs Orr won't let us go 'til we get a maths question right. I hate maths and always pray for an easy one. Sarah-Jane gets two times two and skips away all smiley.

Then Mrs Orr's head turns robot-like towards me. I turn whiter than a stormtrooper, imagining her eyes turning red, and firing a laser-bolt of a question at me that even Obi-Wan Kenobi would have trouble deflecting, "Darryl, seven times seven?"

Phew, the force is with me today. Seven's my favourite number, but I still take a sneaky glance at the tables chart behind her. It's not really cheating 'cos I know the answer and besides I can't see the sum anyway, 'cos her mop of blue hair's blocking it.

"Erm..." I pause dramatically, as if my weekend depends on it. "Forty-nine?"

"Wrong," snaps Mrs Orr, almost before I even finish answering the question.

"Am not," I protest, knowing that on this occasion, I'm definitely right.

Her robotic head tilts slowly towards the chart, just her head mind, the rest of her body doesn't move an inch. It just seems to bob up and down, as she scans the chart,

149

finally stopping as her eyes zoom in on the sum she's looking for, "Only joking, my dear, off you pop."

I don't need to be told twice and I edge past a terrified-looking, but still a bogy-eating Peter, wishing him all the best with a knowing nod, which I reckon is far better than a handshake.

Once outside, I run as fast as my little legs and Snoopy trainers can carry me, accidentally whacking Sarah-Jane's pink lunchbox, with my Muppet one as I go. Sarah-Jane calls me something I don't quite hear. "Smelly girl," I call back anyway. She starts crying but that's not my fault, girls seem to cry a lot for no reason.

I get home in record time and race through the house, dumping my lunchbox and collecting my pocket money all without stopping.

Back outside, this time in the back garden, I grab my BMX that waits patiently in the shed for me, like the Millennium Falcon waiting in the space dock for Han Solo, 'til he needs it to jump into light speed to get away from the evil clutches of the Empire.

My bike's class, it's got fork wheels, which Martin, my brother, calls 'fuck wheels,' when no one else is around to hear him. Mam shouted at me when I said it, everyone else just laughed.

Flying up our drive I notice a no-longer tearful Sarah-Jane walking by sticking her tongue out, which distracts me long enough to hit the metal wotsit that the gates bolt to and off I tumble. Sarah-Jane laughs so I spring back up, pretending that it didn't hurt and seeking revenge. My scuffed knee pops out through my ripped corduroys and she runs off, all giggly, shouting 'H-e-l-p,' like Penelope Pitstop. Luckily for her, she makes it to the alleyway, where bikes and spaceships aren't allowed to go.

"I'll get you back," I vow, sounding a little too like Dick Dastardly, when I've always seen myself more like Peter Perfect.

"See you tomorrow," she calls back, still giggling.

Five minutes later I'm shopping for my cinema club goodies. I take extra care carrying them back but still manage to drop my coke can on the road, only once though. Back at home I search the house for a good place to hide my coke, settling for the freezer 'cos Martin stole it last week and he'd never find it in there.

"What're you doing in there, son?" asks Dad as he puts his workbag down on the kitchen table. "Nowt," I reply almost falling inside.

Dad notices the hole in my knee and asks what happened. I try my best to explain and naturally pin the entire blame on Sarah-Jane. He just gives me a knowing nod, "Women eh?" he says and I reply saying "Aye, women," not really sure what he meant or whether or not I was supposed to say anything at all in reply.

"Give 'em here then," he says reaching for the needle box.

Twenty minutes later I'm tucking my newly patched-up corduroys into my red Wellington boots 'cos Dad wants some help digging the garden so he can plant stuff, 'cos he makes his own vegetables. While I'm waiting for Dad I notice him putting his wallet into the old cupboard-type thing Grandad gave us. The one nobody likes but we're not allowed to throw out. Dad said his wallet's got his driving licence in, but no money. I was going to put this on my list for school but then Dad said it's not really a new discovery 'cos he never has any money in it.

"Have you seen the letter that was in here?" he asks.

151

"No," I reply, "Have you seen me Meccano?"

"Try your wardrobe," he suggests.

"Have you lost something, love?" asks Mam's voice from somewhere in the kitchen.

"No love," replies Dad and "Just me Meccano," I call back.

"Try your wardrobe, pet," replies Mam.

1st Weekend Discovery:
Chewbacca's Been Living In Our Garden For Months.

Outside, I dig for ages and just before Mam calls us in for tea I find my Chewbacca figure I thought Jimmy Passman had nicked last summer and Dad digs up a couple of marbles. "Give them to your Mam," he says, "she lost hers ages ago." I never even knew she played and she doesn't seem that bothered when I give her them. She just stares at Dad the way she did when Martin poisoned my goldfish with her posh perfume she got from Avon.

"That's something else I can add to my list, along with everything else," she says. Dad doesn't reply, I think he's pretending to read his newspaper, so I speak instead, "We have to do a list for school," I offer.

"That's nice, dear," she says patting me on the head on her way back to the kitchen.

2nd Weekend Discovery:
Taylors Don't Share Their Food With Anybody.

At teatime we have to sit down at the table and Martin gets his sulky face on. "You look like you've lost five pence and found half a penny," says Dad. Then when Mam asks what's wrong, Martin whinges like a baby 'cos he wants to watch *Grange Hill*. I don't see what all the fuss is about 'cos it's all about school and he hates school more than me.

Mam brings beef bourguignon out for me and Martin and then an empty plate for Dad with an envelope on it. I hate beef bourguignon, "Can I have the same as Dad?" I ask, which makes everyone laugh except Mam, so I quickly get on with my dinner quietly.

Dad makes himself a chip buttie, which naturally catches Martin's eye and takes his mind right off the tele, "Daaad, can I have one of yah chips?"

Dad moves his plate away from Martin's evil clutches that were hovering just above his plate, "Sorry son, I'm a Taylor and Taylors don't share their food with anybody."

3rd Weekend Discovery:
Tricia Yates Is Gorgeous.

Martin gives up and asks if he could sleep at his mate's house instead. Dad says no, but Mam disagrees, "Your Dad'll drop you off."

"Cool," replies Martin, pushing me away from the sink, even though it's my turn to wash. I'm still drying when he splashes me with dirty dishwater and disappears upstairs singing an Elvis melody. I don't mind too much though, 'cos while we were doing the pots I discovered why he liked *Grange Hill*, it's 'cos Tricia Yates is gorgeous.

I dry the last of the pots ear-wigging to Mam and Dad. They're whispering in the dining room about a court, where you can go for a drink and a drive. It sounds like we might be going on a trip. Then Mam asks what'd happen if Dad lost his driving licence, but he doesn't reply and she lets out a big sigh before stomping towards the kitchen.

"You forgot to wash this," says Mam, slamming my

153

lunchbox onto the worktop just as I'd reassumed my position by the sink. I explain that the chief washer-upper *has* left the kitchen, but get lumbered anyway, despite my best 'that's not fair,' routine, which just seems to fall on deaf ears, as she slips outside for a crafty fag.

Following Mam's example, I drop my lunchbox into the bowl from a great height, hoping to break it, so I'd get a *Star Wars* one like all of my friends, but I just get drenched instead.

The telephone rings loudly in the hall and Dad answers saying our number instead of 'hello', which is really silly 'cos they must know our number already to ring us. When he finishes, he shouts up to Martin to hurry up and then brings his cup into the kitchen asking me to wash it for him, "Oh and tell yah mam I've been called out."

The cup's still warm and half full, so I take a gulp, but spit it out. It tastes horrible. Tinker comes in meowing and licking her lips, so I offer it to her. She sniffs it and pretty much makes the same face I'd just made.

She meows again when I open a carton of orange juice without asking. I take a good gulp to wash away the horrible coffee taste. Tinker licks her lips again, so I pour some into her bowl, as a kind of experiment. I didn't think cats generally liked orange juice but she seems to enjoy it, so I give her some more and then when that's gone, I give her some more.

4th Weekend Discovery:
Geordie The Dog Doesn't Just Chase Boro Fans.

I collect my bike, "Dad's been called out," I say to Mam, who was by now on to her third crafty fag. "Again?" she says. "Dad's been called out," I repeat and then speed off, in search of anyone playing out nearby.

I pedal as fast as I can past the corner, where Ginger-Paul's dog, Geordie, sits. Ginger-Paul reckons he's trained him just to chase Boro fans but as I turn the corner I see Geordie chasing Mr Bell's milk float while he's collecting his money.

Geordie eventually gives up, turning his attention instead to the stray cat that lives in the school field somewhere. Of course the cat is way too fast for Geordie and it's over the metal fence before I can say 'Jack Robinson' and Geordie crashes against it. It must have hurt 'cos he was going at some speed when he hit it and now he seems to be madder than ever. He spies me watching the whole show from the other end of the street and charges after me. I'm off like a shot, I don't want to end up like Peter's older brother, the one who used to pick on anyone who was a little bit different but then stopped when Geordie nearly bit his ear off. Everyone started to call him 'Arthur' after that, not really sure why though, 'cos his name's Kevin.

Anyway, I make it to the safety of the gate we climb over that leads to the school field and heave my bike over just in time. I thought Geordie was going to rip my back wheel off. He sits by the gate for a while but loses interest when he realises that I'm not going back anytime soon.

I pedal round the corner of our classroom to where we often hang out and find Peter sat on the grass with some bigger boys, including Ginger-Paul. They're talking about girls for some reason and Ginger-Paul asks if we've seen any wobblers. I'm not really sure what he means, but Peter swears blind he has, so I do too. Chances are, if he's seen one, I will have too, 'cos we're in the same class.

"Do yahs even know what wobblers are?" asks Ginger-Paul sniggering and I get a bit embarrassed and my cheeks tingle.

"You haven't seen any, have yahs?"

"Probably," I shrug, "Me mam always has wobblers when me dad comes home late from the pub." They all laugh, so I laugh too.

5th Weekend Discovery:
Orange Juice Doesn't Like Our Cat.

As I get home, Mam's down on all fours scrubbing at a large orange stain on the carpet. It turns out that although Tinker seemed to like orange juice, orange juice didn't seem to like her, or blend in well with Mam's new cream-coloured carpet Uncle Michael put down in the hall.

"Try Dad's Hai Karate, it gets most things out." I suggest, which raises Mam's eyebrow a bit, "How would you know that?" she asks.

At one point or another, I've pretty much dabbed Hai Karate on most things including Tinker, but I can't really tell her that so I change the subject quickly.

"Don't worry about Dad's driving licence, he keeps it in a safe place; I wrote it down on my list."

My plan seems to work, "What list?" she asks looking up from the carpet.

"My list of discoveries for school, doesn't anyone listen to me?"

I stomp halfway up the stairs, "Clean your room, while you're up there, pet," shouts Mam, so I slow down and then the phone rings, which gives me a good reason to turn back and tune in, when Mam starts to whisper.

"I think Barry's gone to see Michael, there's been a bit

156

of a kafuffle and he's moved out of Mandy's. Apparently he's decided to come out of the closet, after all this time."

6th Weekend Discovery:
American's Talk Funny.

When Mam finally finishes waffling on about stuff I don't really understand, I ask her what a closet is.

"Nosey-parker. Hasn't anyone ever told you that listening to other people's conversations is rude?" "Yes, you," I reply, which makes her laugh and then she explains it's what American's call a wardrobe.

"Oh," I reply, wondering just how long Uncle Michael's actually been in the wardrobe and whether or not he happened to find my Meccano while he was in there.

7th Weekend Discovery:
You Can't Put Coke Cans In Our Microwave.

The next morning I discover you can't put coke cans in our microwave, even on defrost. As the sparks fly everywhere I panic, worrying that it's going to explode so I pull the plug out and run away. Naturally I come back soon after, 'cos I'd forgotten my coke.

At the cinema Sarah-Jane offers to kiss me for a bite of my Curly-Wurly. "I'm a Taylor and Taylors don't share their food with anybody," I explain with a smile, the same way Dad had done with Martin. Sarah-Jane didn't seem to agree with the Taylor food sharing policy and kicked me just above my ankle, in more or less the exact same place that Steven Powlowski had kicked me with his new DMs, when he thought I'd nicked his pocket guide to tanks. When I told him it was Jimmy Passman he kicked me again and called me a grass.

Sarah-Jane's golden pigtails disappear into the foyer and then Martin and his mate comes up to me laughing 'cos I'd been beaten up by a girl. I get the last laugh though when he snatches my coke can out of my hand and opens it.

8th Weekend Discovery:
Freddie Mercury Doesn't Like Fish.

Dad went all the way to Southampton and back for the football. He came back with Uncle Michael and a Beta-Max video. He was only meant to bring fish and chips.

"Tea up kids," he shouts and I limp to the table. "What's up with you, son?" he asks so I explain about Sarah-Jane kicking me.

"Whereabouts?" he asks looking down at my leg. "At the cinema," I reply, just as Martin sits down, still wearing his coke-stained top.

"Looks like we've all been in the wars," says Uncle Michael. He has a black eye and a cut lip.

"Did a girl hit you too?" I enquire before tucking into my tea.

"Not quite," he replies.

Everyone has fish, except for me and Uncle Michael, which I thought was quite interesting, "Don't you like fish Uncle Michael?" I ask.

"No kidda, I prefer sausage," he replies in a strange voice, kind of higher than usual and he looks at Dad when he answers instead of me, "Me too," I reply anyway.

"Enough!" snaps Dad and he stabs his fork into a big chunk of his fish and then points it at me. "You'll marry Sarah-Jane, whether you like it or not and after twenty odd years or so, it'll more-than-likely be the latter, but you'll do it anyway, 'cos it's the normal thing to do! Here have some of me fish, it's good for you."

158

"But I don't like fish," I protest.

Dad just ignores me and gives Uncle Michael a funny stare, kind of like what Mam does, only not quite as evil. "Part of your problem is listening to that weird new music like Culture Club," he says. "I mean the guy wears make-up for God sake."

"I suppose you'd prefer it if I listened to some proper manly bands like Queen!" says Uncle Michael.

"Exactly," replies Dad through a mouthful of battered Cod.

"Firstly my dear supportive brother, *I* don't have a problem and secondly, I think you'll find Freddie Mercury isn't that keen on *fish* either." This was news that seems to take Dad by surprise, "Never," he replies swallowing his fish.

9th Weekend Discovery:
Beta-Max Videos Are The Latest Thing In Home Entertainment.

After a long moment of nothing but the sound of chewing, Dad speaks a little softer, "Eh, how's about we set the video up later and tape *Doctor Who*?" It sounds like a great idea to me, although Mam doesn't agree. She had up until that point been sat quietly eating her tea like Martin, "Do you really think a stupid video's going to help things?" she snaps.

"It's the latest thing in home entertainment and we've got one right at the beginning of the technical revolution," explains Dad.

"That might well be, but I bet it's not technically advanced enough to take us shopping on a Friday or for days out in the summer!"

"Not in front of the kids, love," says Dad, almost in a whisper.

Mam leaves the table taking her plate and Martin's with her, even though he wasn't quite finished, "You weren't thinking of the kids when you got…" the rest of her sentence disappears with the rest of her into the kitchen, replaced by the loud scraping of dirty plates and left over chips and stuff landing in the bin. Dad follows her in, asking Uncle Michael if he wants a cup of coffee.

"Try using milk instead of whiskey, for a change," suggests Mam. I wonder if that's why it tasted funny when I tried it.

"Alright love, you've made your point," says Dad clattering around for a jug. I run away when he tries to use the microwave to boil the milk.

10th Weekend Discovery:
Doctor Who Doesn't Die; He Just Gets Younger.

This evening at about quarter to six, my life changes forever in a way that I never thought possible. I discover that nothing lasts forever, not even Tom Baker.

"Why has his face changed?" I ask all confused.

"Because he's regenerated, love."

"Will I regenerate?"

"No love,"

"Will Dad?"

"I should be so lucky."

I discover that Doctor Who never dies; he just gets younger.

As the names roll on the screen at the end, Uncle Michael suggests going to the pub. Dad looks at Mam staring at him with her evil eyes that have the ability to burn your face off if she looks at you long enough, "Er, not tonight, mate," he replies.

160

"How about you kidda, do yah fancy a vodka and coke?" he jokes.

"No thanks, I'm not allowed coke anymore," I explain.

It's Sunday and I'm making a 'for sale' sign for Dad's Cortina, as punishment for breaking the microwave, when Uncle Michael announces right out of the blue that he's moving to Brighton to be 'among his own people'. I find this quite confusing, 'cos I always thought he supported Boro, like the rest of us, no wonder Dad's upset.

Uncle Michael looks at the sign I've just painted and likes it that much, he decides to buy Dad's car, on the strength of it.

"I'll get the microwave repaired with your commission," says Dad before taking Uncle Michael out for a 'goodbye pint.'

That night Mam sends me to bed early 'cos she wants to watch the *Eurovision Song Contest* even though, according to the *Radio Times*, it's not on 'til next week.

As I'm reading my *Eagle* annual under the covers with my torch I hear a knock on the front door. I tiptoe over to the window and see Grandad's car parked outside so I sneak downstairs for a listen. I hear Mam saying something about packing, so maybe we're going on a surprise trip after all. Then I hear footsteps heading my way so I rush back upstairs to bed.

On Monday morning, Dad walks us to school wearing his best suit, it's actually his only suit too but he calls it his best one. Everyone's pointing and laughing at us, it's so embarrassing I don't even ask him why he's wearing it, but I think he's entered a competition and is being judged or summat. Martin walks about ten paces in front of us pretending that he's not with us and then disappears into

161

the schoolyard. It's not that easy for me 'cos Dad's holding my hand and leads me all the way to the gate.

"Whatever 'appens son, you know I love you both, don't you." He gives me a big hug and then pats me on the head before rushing off in search of the 263 bus to town.

After Mrs Orr has done the register, she introduces us to a lady who's come to see how good our school is. Sarah-Jane gets picked, yet again, to take the register back to the secretary's office. I never get picked; it's so unfair. When Sarah-Jane returns we start our weekend reports. I'm after Peter, "Very good, but please do try and stop picking your nose, there's a good lad."

I take a deep breath; Sarah-Jane sticks her tongue out at me, I return the gesture and then present my weekend discoveries, recounting every detail, trying my best not to leave anything out. I only get about halfway through, telling them about Freddie Mercury not liking fish, when Mrs Orr interrupts me, "Er, well done, Darryl."

"But I haven't finished yet," I protest.

"There's still more people waiting to do their reports," she explains and reluctantly I sit down.

Our lady visitor decides she's seen enough and leaves with a full notepad and Sarah-Jane punches me really hard on my arm, she never even says why.

About the author

Graham currently divides his time between working for the Local Authority and volunteering with several organisations in varying roles including Foster Carer. In his spare time he runs Good Guy Publishing (a web-based company specialising in electronic publishing, providing help and support to anyone interested in creative writing). Graham's interest in writing began at an early age, and is inspired in part by stories and events he remembers from his childhood.

In Fields of Butterfly Flames

Steve Wade

A St. Bernard pup, my instant pal, he bounded straight to me from the litter of four and the mama dog when I went to collect him. Hardly weaned that evening I brought him home. He didn't last long. Two days later I came in from working the fields to find his little bedraggled body floating in the rusty barrel-drum. On the ground beside the barrel, a garden rake with congealed blood and white dog hairs clinging to its steel teeth.

The instant thrumming that started up in my head gave way to petrified anger as I pressed his sopping and lifeless carcase to my face. The heightened doggy smell pervaded my senses and the freezing wetness soaked through my overalls, chilling me beyond chillness. And there I knelt, shivering and snivelling next to the unused outhouse until the September evening closed, my little pal's remains in my arms, the uneven, stony earth biting into my knees.

The moon threw a bony light across the land. The same ghostly luminosity I remembered playing with the elongated shadows a year before. That terrible night Dale never came home. In the pre-dawn light I found him – what was left of our second born – our only surviving son.

Numbed and helpless, I pushed to my feet and headed for the house, in my arms the St. Bernard puppy I hadn't yet named.

Shona was where I knew she'd be, at the kitchen table. Spread before her like tarot cards, family photos taken from the albums featuring Dale, many of them with sides sheared into curved contours where she'd long ago cut out the images of Robert, our eldest, cancelling him as though he, Robert, had never been. As if, by denying Robert's

163

life, she could erase what he'd done to our family and our family home.

In the photos Dale as an infant; Dale's first steps; Dale red-faced pedalling a tricycle on his third birthday; Dale sitting atop the grey Shetland colt; Dale at the seaside; his first Communion, his Confirmation; Dale through a smile that wasn't a smile blowing out eighteen candles on a birthday cake; his nineteenth and twentieth birthdays. And in Shona's hand, as usual, the photo of a cake featuring a Batman motif and the number 21 – the birthday Shona had insisted we celebrate in Dale's absence.

With the dead pup cradled in my arms, I waited for Shona to release the photo her thumbs caressed. She didn't. I clenched tight my own eyes and shook my head in a futile effort to shake away the images that wouldn't leave me alone: Shona bundling the St. Bernard pup into the barrel. Her maddened, contorted features as she used the garden rake to batter and plunge the screaming and terrified animal beneath the drowning waters.

With bile rising into my throat, I turned from her and for the living room.

In the living room I placed the pup's body on the rug before the hearth, scrunched up some old newspapers and got a fire going to dry out his coat before burial in the morning.

Over the next few weeks, for the best part, I avoided Shona. Did only the necessary jobs to be done with the cattle in the fields and the milking parlour; freeing me with the time I needed to devote to a special project.

The evening I'd been working towards arrived. Only a month since the pup's drowning, and not fully a year since Dale went away, my gut told me Shona still needed way more time. I guessed it'd be this way. That's why I'd spent the last few weeks getting the outhouse ready for the new arrival: put in aluminium window frames with dark, frosted glass and inside shutters, took care of all those areas where draughts might sneak in, and I got hold of a big wicker basket with blankets where he could sleep. The inside walls I re-plastered, put in a toilet and sink, rewired the electricity, warmed the drying plaster with a small heater and stuck in a small cooker and a mini fridge. The old sofa I'd kept stored in the barn would do me.

The renovated outhouse would also give me a place to escape from Shona – lately she'd been depressing me like I never thought possible. Far more cosy in the house naturally, but my new pal and me would do fine out there. And as for Shona coming mooching around the outhouse, I wasn't concerned. She seldom left the house anymore.

Because my new pal would be quite young, my plan was to stay with him nights, right up until I felt Shona was ready to accept him in the house. No way I would have left him on his own on that cold stone floor beneath those rafters at any rate. Not at night-time.

Shona wouldn't be bothered by my absence. Truth is, we hadn't slept in the same bed these past months.

Anyway, I could hardly contain my excitement that first evening. Finally, there he was safe in his basket where I left him. Just how I imagined it. I'd picked him up early that morning. Drove over a hundred miles to get him. He wailed and whimpered for hours for his mama. That was the toughest part of it. He refused to take food and drink, his eyes retreated from mine whenever I got too close, and his body froze like a lamb with hypothermia.

I left a bowl of milk near his basket, and in another bowl some of the reheated rabbit stew I'd cooked up especially the night before. He'd come round. As I said, he was young yet.

I was right. Although, after three or four days, I'd been starting to doubt my convictions, and came very close to bundling him back into the Pajero, driving back to where I picked him up and depositing him in the street. But one day when I came in from the fields at lunchtime, he toppled out of his basket and padded right up to me.

"Hey," I said. "Hello. There's a good boy. You ready to be my friend now?"

He nodded up at me, a tiny even-toothed smile on his face. "Yeah," he said and jerked up his arms, like a game he was maybe used to playing. "Yeah," he repeated.

"Okay," I said, and playfully copied his arm movements. I then ruffled his curly head, his hair the same russet-red as Dale's, except Dale's had been straight. One of the reasons I'd chosen him: his hair.

Just like the boys when they were kids, my little pal was temperamental. One moment he was giggling and turning the potato chips on his plate into impromptu cars and planes and making engine noises, the next he was blubbering for his mama again. But as soon as I told him we were going to drive the tractor around the fields, he forgot all about his mama. He even put on some of the clothes I'd left out for him. Dale's clothes: striped trousers, a batman T-shirt, and a pair of blue wellies, stuff that Shona'd kept for a million years. She's a hoarder. Shona. Holds onto everything.

Sitting upfront in the tractor cabin, he could have been one of the boys. He pointed at the screaming seagulls the way the boys used to, and giggled at the blades churning up the earth; and his hair smelt just the way theirs did, of shampoo and vitality.

The only time he got a bit confused was when I called him 'Dale'. He stuck out his lower lip, cried, and told me his real name. I eased down on the brakes, killed the

166

engine, and explained that we were playing a pretend game. He could pretend I was his daddy, couldn't he? And I could pretend his name was Dale.

"You're not my daddy," he said, his back pressed to the tractor door, his features a knot of confusion and fear, the way he appeared the day he arrived.

"No, of course I'm not." I ruffled his untidy hair. "How about 'Pa'? Why don't you call me Pa?"

He made no answer, but his crying stopped. He twisted round, his face and palms pressed against the glass.

"Look," he said, pointing at the darkening sky. "A nail."

Puzzled at first by what he meant, I got it when he glanced and giggled a gurgly giggle at his own wiggling thumb. A fingernail. He saw the quarter moon set in the charcoal-blue sky as a fingernail clipping. What a clever kid. He and Dale really might have been the same boy. Despite being two years younger, Dale was way smarter than Robert. Always was.

For my little pal and me the following weeks fell into a routine, a routine I wished could've lasted forever: once I'd milked the cattle, put them out to graze in the low fields, weather permitting, and fed and watered the bay mare, I'd return to Dale – the newest Dale – who'd already be up, sleepy-eyed and waiting, prepare his coco-pops and juice, get him cleaned up, and then out to the fields, the two of us, where we'd talk, laugh and sing our way through the morning and into the evening in the tractor cabin or mucking about the fields.

Soon, with the limited daylight, the crops on a go-slow, and Halloween drawing near, there was less reason for us to be in the fields. Just as well. I was worried about the effects the drop in temperature might be having on the lad. This concern turned into obsession. The old two-bar

167

electric heater and small blow heater hardly made a difference in our converted outhouse: our home. So I pulled out from a load of junk in the cowshed a baseboard heater I'd long ago forgotten about.

But despite the three heaters turned up full, the place never reached room temperature. Must have been the stone floor and the original dampness. So when little Dale began coughing this nasty cough that sounded like he might tear his throat, I knew the time had come. Time to introduce him to Shona.

Completely hidden by the band of conifers, I could make out Shona's familiar seated figure in the square of light at the kitchen table when I emerged along the dirt path clutching Dale's hand. Not knowing for sure how Shona might react when she saw the boy, I warned him that the lady we were going to visit wasn't well. She cried a lot, I told him. Sometimes she screamed. And her eyes were big, like an owl's eyes. But there was no need for him to be afraid. After all, I was with him. I'd never let anything happen to him. His pa would protect him.

"Shona," I said after I wiped my feet across the worn straw doormat. "I've got a surprise for you."

Just as I'd foreseen, Shona initially ignored me. Her maddened eyes kept right on scouring the photos before her, as if she might yet detect the missing minutiae to undo the unanswerable.

"Son," I said, directing the boy in front of me by the shoulders. "This is your... this is Shona."

In my palms I felt his resistance like the first strike of a brown trout. That sense of being hyper-connected to another living creature, its pulse firing along the fishing line and coursing through you so that you and it are indistinguishable: two beings one soul.

I smiled reassuringly down at his upturned face, his

mouth shaping the word 'Pa' – I was almost sure of it.

The terrible sound that peeled from Shona then was the scream I'd last heard the morning I came through the open kitchen door, Dale's lifeless body draped across my shoulders in a fireman's lift, branded around his neck the hanging mark left by the blue rope I sometimes used as a makeshift halter for the bay mare.

"You're frightening him, Shona. Please."

Wedged between the counter, where she now stood, and the accidentally overturned kitchen table, she shook her head, her swollen eyes the predatory eyes of a cornered beast.

Dale had turned away from her, his whole face clenched, his arms about my leg. I picked him up.

"Pa," he said. "Pa."

About to escape clutching the boy, Shona's frozen face shifted, her attention on the scattered photos lying in the black and white tiled floor. A new terror played in her features. And then she was on her knees, scratching at the photos' corners, gathering them together. But what happened next I could never have foreseen.

Dale indicated he wanted to be put down. He then tottered to Shona, crouched next to her and began to scoop up some of the photos. Shona jerked from him, her head sideways, her eyes jammed in their corners.

My entire being coiled, primed to intervene, as I watched Shona's eyes, bubbles in a spirit level, right themselves slowly as she twisted her face towards Dale. The smile that curled her lips retransforming, returning the once beautiful face that, till then, taunted like a memory of something that never was.

"Who's this?" she asked, her gaze locked to Dale the way a lioness locks onto a grazing gazelle from behind tall grass. "Where did you get him?"

169

"He needs us to look after him," I said. Too soon to even consider using his name on front of Shona. Later. That would come later.

"He's beautiful," she said.

On her knees she opened her arms. Dale hesitated. Twisted round to me. Sweating, I nodded. And, as in a rare vignette, one that doesn't terrify, dreamed under heavy fever, it happened. Dale kind of stumbled forward and fell into Shona's motherly embrace.

"There, there," she said. "Mo chuisle. Mo chuisle mo chroi," using the language of her rural background. *My pulse. Pulse of my heart.*

From that moment, Shona and Dale were as inseparable and steadfast as a successful peach and pear tree grafting.

In the mornings, Shafts of autumn sunlight, through the kitchen window, animated their lively togetherness. Dale sang nursery rhymes with Shona, his piping voice blending with the warbling and trilling that poured in from the hazel trees and yew hedging in the garden. Evening times they sat together at the kitchen table making fairy cakes and gingerbread men. And from a book I hadn't seen for years, Shona read to him tales of ants and eagles, wolves and lions, foxes and crows. Dale's eyes swelled bigger than a puppy's, his laughing voice pre-empting words spoken by fabled creatures whose lives he already knew and relived during Shona's reading.

All seemed renewed. Like the imminent catastrophes magically overridden in those fantastic fables, beauty and harmony to the world had been restored. And yet inside my stomach there bubbled something evil, a warning that wouldn't leave me alone. And I, in turn, refused the temptation to leave Dale alone with Shona. Perhaps because she insisted Dale call her by her name. While she

170

only ever addressed Dale as 'love' or 'a stor mo chroi' – *darling of my heart.*

Could be that I imagined it, but there was another thing: in Shona's eyes an occasional glint that reminded me of certain dogs I've owned or encountered over the years. A wild look, an emptiness that cancelled every trace of thousands of years' domesticity would sizzle in their canine eyes. The eye-glint that flashed before the attack, the sudden, unexpected snap and snarl when teeth connected with outstretched hand.

Never would I allow her to be alone with him, I vowed. Not ever.

The dairy herd lowing in the barn to be milked in the early mornings I tried to ignore. Not until Dale was up and finished his breakfast did I leave the house, with Dale in my arms or tottering sleepily beside me. The big basket from the outhouse I'd removed and placed in the milking parlour. While I got the milking machine going and hooked up the teat cups, Dale curled up under his blankets, asked endless questions, sang snatches of nursery rhymes and usually fell asleep.

Shona's endless pleading, it was, that altered this routine.

"A little mite," she kept at me. "And you dragging him out into the cold. Is it mad you are?"

"Good for the lad," I said. "It'll toughen him up. Turn him into a hardy soul."

But Shona wouldn't leave off her badgering. And she seemed to be deteriorating again. The signs were obvious. Even pulled out the photo album one afternoon.

Finally, I relented. No choice. But not before I'd re-explained to Dale that Shona wasn't well. And that sometimes adults who are unwell do things they don't mean to. Like hurt people. I gave him a spare key to the

171

outhouse, showed him how to use it and how to lock himself inside should he ever feel that Shona was going to hurt him. There he was to stay till I came to get him.

"Do you understand? You come here; lock yourself in like this, and I'll be here soon. Okay?"

He got it. I could tell. Such a bright kid.

Unconvinced, however, about Shona's mental state, I hurried in from the parlour with beating temples and knotted stomach at what horror scene awaited me that first day I left him alone with her. And this pattern I continued at half-hourly intervals throughout the day and days that followed during the week. My dinner during that period I could hardly look at.

But just when the beating in my head began to ease, and a healthy appetite usurped my twisted stomach, I emerged from the conifer grove one evening to a sight that caught me in the solar plexus. Hot, bitter bile erupted from my throat and spilled through my lips. Enervated, I drew my sleeve across my mouth and squinted towards the house.

In the kitchen window a shimmering orange light centred on the ledge replaced the normal light: the pumpkin they'd been carving that afternoon. Absent were Dale and Shona's figures.

Into an impulsive sprint I broke and reached the house in seconds.

"Dale," I shouted as I pounded through the house. "Shona! Dale!" I heard my detached voice bellowing, while I pulled open doors, crashed into furniture and fittings and tore away crumpled bedclothes.

Gone – both of them. What had she done? What had I let that fiend do?

In my urgency to get back down the stairs, I slipped. Something detonated inside my ankle, sending a metallic sheet of pain exploding across my vision. Working my way back onto my feet at the bottom of the stairs, a follow-up explosion, raw and crimson, erupted behind my eyes, buckling me like a shot hind. Pushing through the blinding pain, I dragged myself over the floor and to the kitchen. There I summoned greater willpower and strength than I could have imagined I possessed, and pressed, pulled and pushed my way to one leg.

Using the sweeping-brush as a crutch, I tried to steal myself against the inevitable horror forming in my head. The barrel-drum. I had to get to the barrel-drum.

Every movement down the three steps from the kitchen into the yard brought intolerable sledgehammer blows slamming against my ankle. I clenched my teeth and released intermittent growls: ugly, guttural sounds, the snarls of a creature in deep distress, or a murderer, maybe, wedded to the moment when his blade sears flesh, and blood splashes and gushes hotly, soaking his killing hands and soul with satiated lust and love.

Too far from the shimmering light in the kitchen window, I could just about make out the palette that acted as a makeshift lid removed and resting against the barrel's side.

Fractured images of the drowned pup; of Dale's stiffened body hanging from the outhouse rafters, and of Robert, almost two years before him, in the floor of that same outhouse, his head half-blown away, my Magnum hunting rifle next to him, bleeding his life away in my lap. The images splashed about among the swirling pain.

The barrel, half-hidden by the shade thrown beneath the eaves of the low-pitched roof, made it impossible to see inside the container. So I plunged my arm through the blackened water up to my shoulder. The Arctic coldness cutting into my flesh, right through to the bone marrow, gave instant respite from the intolerable burning flailing my ankle.

Empty. The barrel was empty.

Relieved, confused, terrified, I snapped my head backwards at the night sky and cursed the nothingness. The sickening pain shooting from my ankle to my head I welcomed.

Robert and Dale dead. Somehow, as their father, their deaths belonged to me. And now I had surely killed Dale again.

More than pain, I too deserved death. But before I accepted and administered the self-inflicted punishment, I had to behold Dale's twisted and slain form. My instincts pushed me on through the yard towards the outhouse.

Unaccustomed to strange movements once they'd been housed for the night, the cattle hoofed about uneasily in the barn, grunting and complaining. The bay mare, from her stable, whinnied and blew for my attention. I limped onward towards the outhouse.

Drawing near I thought I could see a sliver of light slicing through the window shutter. I pushed on harder.

Scrabbling in my overalls for the keys when I reached the door, I could swear I heard a voice or voices whispering inside. I stopped. I listened… Yes. Shona's voice and, Jesus, it couldn't be… could it? I eased down the door handle and peered through the gap.

Silence now. Then from behind the door…

"Boo!" Dale.

I fell backwards, renewed pain lacerating my ankle. But I didn't care.

"Dale," I said. "Dale. You're… You're okay!"

"Pa fall down, Shona," he said twisting round to her. "Pa fall down." And he came to me, his little hands gripping my arm, his face fully concerned, in a huge effort

174

to drag me to my feet.

"Oh my God," Shona said, stepping into the night. "Are you okay?"

Shona's immediate suggestion that she call an ambulance I countered.

"No, Shona. "I'll be fine. Really. It's just a sprain. Ice. You guys help me inside and, eh, ice. From the mini fridge. Ice." Ensuring Shona was fully focused my way, I allowed my eyes to jump in Dale's direction. I raised my eyebrows and nodded. A look I hope she'd get.

Her eyes alighting on Dale narrowed. She pursed her lips. She got it. Neither one of us needed the authorities sniffing around the farm.

Once they helped me inside, and Shona made up an ice-pack, placed a mug of tea before me and explained how Dale had brought her by the hand to what he called 'the uddy house', she and Dale sat down together at the table and got on with what they'd clearly been doing before I arrived.

"Look," she said to Dale. "I found another one that fits."

Dale clapped his hands and giggled.

Sticking the cut up photos back together. Christ. She'd kept the images of Robert. She never could discard anything.

"Oh look," she said. "There you are with Robert, Dale. The day we had the picnic by the lake. The day it snowed in March."

Another explosion rocketed skyward in my head. But this time a fireworks explosion crowded with an unbearable feeling of pure joy. But as the coloured trails and sparks burned away, they took with them my fleeting elation. Deposited in its place despair – instant, utter and complete.

Robert. Robert and Dale. Dale and Robert. Never were two lads more inseparable than our boys. Two years between them, they were best buddies from the day we brought Dale home from the hospital. So close were they, Dale stuck right by his big brother when Robert got sick, when Robert's head betrayed him, made him think crazy thoughts and do terrible things.

Like that summer, Robert's last summer, he trapped butterflies. Convinced the butterfly swarms were descending on the farm as a locust-plague. He started out by pinning the insects to the old picnic table by the lake with bramble-bush thorns. He'd then place a magnifying glass between them and the sun, his eyes widening, and his nostrils expanding, as he pulled in the wispy smoke plumes rising from the smouldering carcases.

A failure on my part to get the boy help, I admit it. He graduated to trapping butterflies in the hundreds. That's all he did that summer. Trapped them and kept them in an old reptile cage he had in his bedroom. Sometimes he'd set them free in the room and just sit in his computer chair, this look on his face, watching the butterflies flit about, alighting on bookshelves and picture-frames, or thrashing against the window for freedom.

Afraid of the consequences I was. Shona too. We discussed it. We'd work through his troubles as a family.

Too late. I got a call one afternoon from the emergency services to get back quickly to the farm. Shona, Dale and I were at the weekend market operating the vegetable stall. There'd been an accident, the guy on the phone warned.

The flames were still devouring the farmhouse when I pulled up outside the gate to our home: patrol cars, fire brigades and flashing lights. They'd cordoned off the entrance, the police or the firemen. Neighbours had gathered.

"Robert," I shouted at the policemen trying to restrain me from pushing past the bodies and the vehicles. "My son Robert is inside. Please, I have to…"

"He's safe," the sergeant said, his hands on my shoulders. "We have him. He's safe. It's okay." For his own safety, he told me, they had him in one of the cars. He pointed.

I pushed past.

"Excuse me," I said. "My son. Can you let me through, please?" The crowd made way.

"Robert," I said, tugging open the car door. "Robert, are you okay? What happened?"

But Robert was already somewhere else. Wasn't even aware of my presence. His bloated face, crammed with concentration, never shifted from the inferno, the flames flickering in his pupils and dancing on his skin. From his throat a sickening, high-pitched keening caused the guard seated next to him to snap the cuffs attached to their wrists.

"Relax," the young guard said. "Take it easy now."

I frowned at the handcuffs and then at the guard.

"For his own safety," the guard said. "For his safety, sir."

And for Robert's safety, and ours, we finally had him committed for a while, but he talked us into getting the doctor to sign his release. The provision being that he continued to take the prescribed drugs.

Robert fooled us there too.

Twenty-three months. Dale waited twenty-three months before he followed Robert. We failed to read the signs. All summer he'd been talking about how, his next birthday, he'd be exactly the age Robert was when Robert went away. Dale just couldn't cope without him.

Tomorrow. Tomorrow was Halloween. I'd get Shona

177

to drive into town for a Batman outfit. Then, in the evening, we could all head off like a family in Shona's car to some other town – a faraway town, where nobody knew us. Shona would understand. Crowded with compassion now, she was ready to forgive. While I sat in the car with my bandaged ankle, she and Dale could go trick or treating. The perfect day and time to seek out Dale's big brother Robert, lost and lonely out there somewhere, waiting. Waiting for forgiveness.

About the author

A prize nominee for the PEN/O'Henry Award, 2011, and for the Pushcart Prize, 2013, Steve Wade's fiction has been published widely in print and online. His work has been shortlisted among five in the Wasafiri Short Story Prize 2011, nominated for the Hennessy New Irish Writer Prize, and he gained Second Place in the International Biscuit Publishing contest, 2009. His fiction has been published in Bridge House, Crannog, Zenfri Publications, New Fables, Gem Street, Grey Sparrow, Fjords Arts and Literary Review, and Aesthetica Creative Works Annual.

www.stephenwade.ie

There Must Be More

David West

In the mirror I see a trickle of blood start to seep from a cut on the edge of the faint old scar from my father's ring. I rinse off the remaining foam then tear off a small piece of toilet tissue and press it against the cut until the blood starts to congeal. I put on my linen suit. Good! My Round Table pin is in the left lapel. It's important to be seen to be supporting charities and you never know where you're going to meet another member. As my father used to say, before he abandoned us, it's not what you know, it's who you know! I boot up the laptop and check the presentation again. If I can win this project it'll really make me, I'll have arrived, earned my place at the top table! Yep, I've put together a first class presentation as usual. The phone rings.

"Hello, Mr James, your car has arrived."

"Thank you, I'll be down in five minutes." The lift doors open and a porter is there to take my laptop case. The Raj Palace hotel reception is bustling with tourists and businessmen, a cacophony of accents and colour. A party of perhaps a dozen Buddhist monks in orange robes catches my eye. One of them arrests my gaze and approaches me holding out a camera.

"You take photo please?" he smiles.

"I don't have time." I step around him and make my way to the Concierge's desk followed by my eager porter. A pretty young woman with long black hair, brown eyes and wearing a turquoise sari is waiting by the desk.

"Mr James?"

"My name is James Carter, yes."

"Welcome to Delhi Mr James. I am Sarvari, Mr Rao's

179

personal assistant. Mr Rao is very, very much looking forward to meeting you. Our car is outside, this way please." Sarvari opens the back door of a black Mercedes and smiles. I settle into the sumptuous grey leather and look round to check that my laptop bag has been taken by the driver and put in the boot. She and the driver take the front seats and as we set off a tall Sikh hotel doorman salutes us.

We turn left out of the hotel gates and after a few hundred yards reach a junction with a main road. The driver begins blowing his horn and edges out into the traffic. A blue bus with many passengers clinging onto the outside lets us in. I have never seen anything like it; three wheeled yellow and green rickshaws jostle with cars, lorries and motorcycles, everyone hooting. I notice that all the lorries and buses although covered in Sanskrit writing have a large notice on the back saying "Horn Please!" We are passed by a motorcycle carrying a family of five, no six. Only the father is wearing a crash helmet.

"Mr James, the traffic is very good today and I think we will be at the office in very, very good time. I believe this is your first visit to India, yes?"

"Yes, although I hope to spend a lot of time here when we win the contract." She smiles.

At a junction a woman with a baby in her arms gets up from a carpet of filthy cardboard underneath the flyover for the Metro and begins working her way down the queue of traffic with hand outstretched. A few people drop coins into her hand and I am grateful for the tinted glass, I don't think she can see me.

"I am sorry about this Mr James; the police really should do something about these beggars. It is making a very very bad advertisement for India. What must you think?"

180

"Oh don't worry; it's much the same in England you know, just a lot colder." Thankfully the traffic starts to move again. Yes, India is the place to be. There seem to be construction sites on every street. The place is booming. We pass markets and shopping malls, garages, apartment blocks and shanty towns where hovels are built from corrugated iron and plastic sheeting. With some amusement I notice that they are all clustered around electricity pylons and have plugged themselves in, because through gaps in the sheeting I glimpse a television flickering. They do all right. Everywhere dogs seem to be running around barking. A horse drawn cart seems to be out of control and is losing much of its load of cardboard. Then my vision begins to blur.

It's quite sudden. Traffic comes to an abrupt halt. The white apartment building on the right is shaking, cracking and then falling. Dust rises and concrete blocks are tumbling and rolling across the road in front. Jesus, is it a bomb, earthquake? What the hell is happening?

"Oh Mr James, come, come quickly it is an earthquake. Very very bad. It is not safe. The Connaught Hotel is just over there, very nice hotel and new. We will be safe there. Come quickly!"

I follow Sarvari and notice that the driver stays with the car. Good, at least my laptop should be safe.

The Connaught Hotel towers up through the swirling dust, a black glass and steel triumph of modern engineering over nature. I follow Sarvari up some steps and through the rotating door. The cool air makes me shiver, just for a second. She leads me to the lounge area and we sit in leather armchairs around a large coffee table. A waiter approaches her at once and she addresses him in Hindi. She turns and smiles at me.

"Would you like coffee or tea Mr James? I'm afraid

181

we may be stuck here a little while until the road is cleared. I will phone Mr Rao and explain. Perhaps some cake too?"

"Er, yes coffee would be nice. I need something to wake me up; I must be dreaming." Sarvari says a few more words to the waiter who bows and walks away. Then she takes a Blackberry out of her handbag and makes a call. I walk over to the window which has a panoramic view across the chaos. The apartment building is split in two. One part is rubble spewing out over the remnants of a wall and across the road; the other part is still standing like a five story open dolls house. All of life is there, kitchens with tables, fridges and cookers; bedrooms, some with double beds and some smaller ones with bunk beds; bathrooms; dining rooms; lounges. Many of the lounges have shrines to one Hindu god or another. Where are they today I wonder? Movement catches my eye. Some men are scrambling over the rubble with a ladder. They are making their way towards half a stairwell and I can see two children sitting a few steps up from a twenty foot gap before the staircase begins again.

"Mr Rao says that you must not worry Mr James. He will find time to see you today as he very much wants to hear about your experience with the power plants in China. He is very sorry that you have been so inconvenienced by this terrible earthquake. It is quite the worst one to hit Delhi in fifty years they are saying on the news."

"That is kind of him, but look I… I think I ought to go and see if I can help."

"Oh no Mr James, that is a very bad idea. It isn't safe! The police and the army will be here very very soon, I'm sure. They will deal with it. Ah look here is our coffee! Thank you Gupta! And look you see there, there is a digger coming. The road will be cleared soon. You just enjoy your coffee Mr James!"

Sarvari is right, a tracked, back acting excavator is moving across the rubble, looks like a Caterpillar 320C. The men have reached the children now and they are being handed down the ladder. What if there are people under the rubble? The Cat will crush them for sure.

"No I really think I should go and help. There's no sign of the police or army or anything." I turn and walk towards the door but there's a tug on my right arm. Her hand slides down my arm and I feel the pressure of her soft flesh in my hand.

"You must stay here Mr James. The road will be clear soon and Mr Rao is expecting us. What about your beautiful suit and shoes?"

"Perhaps you're right, I don't want... oh what are they doing with the bloody thing now? They'll have the rest of that apartment down if they start digging there!" I drop her hand and rush outside. The swish of the revolving door shuts out the calm coolness of the hotel. The morning heat of Delhi in June assaults me, then the noise. Many more people are rushing around now. Men and women are screaming, calling out names. The digger is scratching away at the rubble, its engine revving with the effort. I scramble across the rubble to it. "Stop!" I bang on the cab window then cross and un-cross my arms in a signal to stop. The driver looks at me blankly. "Does anyone here speak English?" I plead, looking around. There is a second's lull in the screaming then it starts again. "E-N-G-L-I-S-H? Does anyone speak English?"

"Sir, yes sir I am speaking English."

Oh thank God! A short fat man is clambering towards me.

"Look we must listen for people under here," I say pointing down and cupping my ear. "Can you make

183

people quiet and get that digger turned off so that we can listen for people?"

"Sir, yes I am following you. I will try." He turns to go and I grab his hand.

"What is your name? I am James."

"Mr James Sir, yes my name is Alam. I will make quiet and then we will listen."

With an energy and surefootedness which belie his age and build, Alam is rushing around shouting, pointing and cupping his ear. Gradually the noise disperses. There is no such thing as silence in Delhi I have learnt, but as the digger engine stops this gets close to it. I kneel down in the rubble and press my ear into a gap. Nothing! I look up and all around me men, women and children are doing the same. I choose another spot and listen intently. Still nothing! Then there is a shout and everyone is making their way towards a teenage girl who is waving. I get there first, lie down and push my head into a gap in the rubble. Nothing at first, but now I can hear breathing.

"Hello, can you hear me? Keep calm we'll get you out." I start scrabbling at the blocks, broken furniture, shards of glass. Around me people are doing the same. We work as one. When a large block is uncovered hands appear around me and we lift. Then I see a foot. It's in a woman's shoe, a red shoe decorated with beads. Now I see a leg through a ripped sari streaked with blood. As we uncover more I see that the leg must be broken in a dozen places. Hands are working their way along the line of her body. Another large block is lifted to uncover her head. Oh God, that doesn't look good. I feel her neck for a pulse but feel nothing. I check my own neck to remind myself where the pulse should be. Mine is pounding like a piling rig. I check again for her pulse, but nothing. I can still hear breathing though, and now sobbing too.

"Alam, can we lift her now please?" We all gently lift together and curled up tight beneath her broken body is a child. The child's eyes blink and the gentle sobbing turns to screaming as it takes in the scene and its dead mother. The child's screams echo off the memory of my screams from a lifetime ago, cut short by the clout of my father's hand before he slammed the front door on my childhood for ever. A wall collapses inside me too and something breaks through. It rises slowly at first, slowly but insistently, then welling up through my stomach and chest, spurting, flowing, choking me, drowning me, I gasp for breath but there are only tears. Great, huge, marbles of tears that haven't seen the light of day for years roll down my dusty cheeks. I lift my hands to my face and see the shreds of skin and blood from tearing at blocks and splinters and broken glass. The tears collect my blood and drip onto the lifeless body beneath me, mixing with her blood and flesh and bone. I am aware of the screaming child being handed back down a chain of helping hands. Then Alam puts his arm around me.

"Sir, Mr James, there must be more. We must keep listening, keep digging. There must be more Mr James, there must be more!"

About the author

David West is a civil engineer who, having had a text book published in 2010, is now trying to turn his newly discovered discipline of writing three hundred words a day into something creative. *There Must Be More* was written for an assignment on the Open University's A215 Creative Writing course. He also enjoyed A363 which focusses on script writing techniques.

Index of Authors

Other Publications by Bridge House

Otherwhere and Elsewhen

Tales of alternative realities

edited by Gill James

Are we alone? Surely not. Do other realities exist? They must
do mustn't they? This can't be it, can it?

If you weren't convinced before, you certainly will be after
you've read this collection of stories that take place in another
time and another space, light years from here. Come read and
discover what happened otherwhere and elsewhen.

"If you love Si-FI then you should defiantly get this. The
Authors have great imaginations and have created some
fantastic worlds."
(*Amazon*)

Order from www.bridgehousepublishing.co.uk

Paperback: ISBN 978-1-907335-23-5
eBook: ISBN 978-1-907335-28-0

Crime After Crime

edited by Debz Hobbs-Wyatt
and Stephen Puleston

Crime writing at its best: strong stories, frighteningly real characters and powerful narratives. This collection is a show-case of talent from new and established writers. Find yourself trapped in the heads of victims pleading for mercy, or the evil minds of cold bloodied serial killers. Whether it's blackmail, obsession or a case of wrong place, wrong time, there is blood. And there is crime. Crime after Crime.

"One of the best collection of crime stories I have come across recently. Let's have more."
(*Amazon*)

Order from www.bridgehousepublishing.co.uk

Paperback: ISBN 978-1-907335-24-2
eBook: ISBN 978-1-907335-26-6

Future plans for Bridge House

We're rationalising our activity a little and going for just one collection a year. This will in the future be by submission rather than competition i.e. no one pays to be considered. So:

- A call will go out each year on 1 January for submissions by 31 March
- Stories will be selected by 30 June
- We'd aim to get book put together ready for marketing by 30 September
- We'll launch on about 15 November (to catch the Christmas markets).

What else will we do?

- We'll have a get-together each year a couple of weeks before Christmas in London
- We'll keep all of our books in print and on Kindle
- We'll always allow authors 25% discount and free shipping on orders of 5 or more books
- There'll be other offers for loyal customers and authors from time to time.

How to keep in touch?

- Keep an eye on the web site www.bridgehousepublishing.co.uk
- Sign up for the newsletter www.bridgehousepublishing.co.uk/bhnewsletter.html
- Follow Debz and Gill on Twitter @BridgehouseDebz @gilljames

Did you know Bridge House has published over 200 authors?